PATTINSON, J.

The emperor stone

THE EMPEROR STONE

THE EMPEROR STONE

James Pattinson

Chivers Press • G.K. Hall & Co.
Bath, Avon, England   Thorndike, Maine USA

This Large Print edition is published by Chivers Press, England, and by G.K. Hall & Co., USA.

Published in 1996 in the U.K. by arrangement with Robert Hale Limited.

Published in 1996 in the U.S. by arrangement with Robert Hale Limited.

U.K. Hardcover ISBN 0-7451-4825-5 (Chivers Large Print)
U.K. Softcover ISBN 0-7451-4837-9 (Camden Large Print)
U.S. Softcover ISBN 0-7838-1626-X (Nightingale Collection Edition)

Copyright © James Pattinson 1993

The right of James Pattinson to be identified as author of this work has been asserted by him in accordance with the Copyright, Designs and Patents Act 1988.

All rights reserved.

The text of this Large Print edition is unabridged.
Other aspects of the book may vary from the original edition.

Set in 16 pt. New Times Roman.

Printed in Great Britain on acid-free paper.

British Library Cataloguing in Publication Data available

Library of Congress Cataloging-in-Publication Data

Pattinson, James, 1915–
   The emperor stone / James Pattinson.
     p. cm.
   ISBN 0-7838-1626-X (lg. print : lsc)
   1. Large type books. I. Title.
[PR6066.A877E47   1996]
823'.914—dc20   95-47883
                                                                                          CIP

Contents

1	Assignment	1
2	Encounter	17
3	Dream	31
4	Asset	44
5	Embarkation	62
6	Bargain	75
7	Temptation	85
8	Help	101
9	Tail	111
10	Search	125
11	Problem	142
12	Argument	157
13	Ride	176
14	Jokers	189
15	Always	207

Contents

1 Assignment 1
2 Encounter 17
3 Dream 31
4 Asset 44
5 Embarkation 62
6 Bargain 75
7 Temptation 85
8 Help 101
9 Talk 111
10 Search 125
11 Problem 142
12 Argument 157
13 Ride 170
14 Jokers 189
15 Always 207

CHAPTER ONE

ASSIGNMENT

With the coming of evening, artillery activity died down. All day there had been desultory firing by the field guns arrayed in the park on the north side of the Presidential Palace, chipping relentlessly away at the fortifications. Mortars had lobbed shells from concealed positions, doing more damage and claiming victims here and there, while snipers had shot at anything that came into their sights.

There had been attacks from helicopter gunships also; but the light anti-aircraft guns on the roof had shot two of the machines down, and this had apparently deterred further action of that description. A couple of elderly Mustang fighter-bombers had joined in, but not very effectively; and this appeared to be about all that the besiegers could muster in the way of air power.

Nevertheless, as Payne and the rest of the defenders knew only too well, the end could not be much longer delayed; the odds were too great and this was the last stand of those still remaining loyal to President Cardona. Indeed, if the palace had not been built originally to serve as a fortress in the event of the need arising as well as a residence for the head of state it would not have held out as long as it had against the forces now attacking it. But it had been under siege for two weeks and no one engaged in its defence could any longer blind himself to the fact that its eventual fall was inevitable.

Yet the defenders would fight on to the last, not so much for reasons of loyalty but because they had little choice except to do so. If they surrendered they could hope for little mercy from the enemy, and it was better perhaps to die from a bullet in the heart or the rending splinter of a shell than swinging at the end of a rope.

Alan Payne was in a similar position and knew that he had been a fool to allow himself to be caught up in such a situation. He had seen it coming months ago, had known he was on the losing side in this ridiculous Central American conflict and ought to get to hell out of it while he still had the chance. For, after all, it was not really his fight; he owed no allegiance to Juan Carlos Cardona; he was there simply to give training in weapon use to the so-called Palace Guard, an élite corps dedicated to the task of protecting the President. It was the remnants of this corps who were now putting up a last forlorn stand in a battle that was to all intents and purposes already lost. And when they went down Payne feared that he would go down with them. What a stupid and pointless end for a man of thirty-two, in the prime of life and as full of vigour as he had ever been! What a waste!

He had learned his trade in the British army, and perhaps he should have stayed in it, making it his career. It might have been better for him. But he had wanted a change, wanted to widen his horizons. And so he had become a soldier of fortune; the term had a romantic ring to it, but there had been precious little romance in fact, though he had earned good money and there had been no shortage of willing employers.

So in the course of time he had come to President Cardona and had worked for him for a year, helping to prop up an increasingly shaky dictatorship. Yet he had never felt any allegiance to the man for whom he was working; it was simply a job for which he was being paid. And Cardona was not the kind of man to command respect; he himself had seized power in a military coup some years ago, had illegally set himself up as unelected president and had done nothing whatever to improve the lot of the common people of his country. In an impoverished state he and his henchmen had lined their own pockets and had maintained a harsh regime by ruthless methods of repression and bloodshed.

Inevitably opposition had grown, ineffective at first but steadily increasing. And what had been no more than a ragged band of guerilla fighters hiding in the jungle had become a force to be reckoned with, a force which had engaged the military in a ceaseless war of attrition and had as time went by drawn to its side even a large body of the regular army itself. Eventually it had become unstoppable.

*   *   *

Payne felt a touch on his arm. The light had become so poor now that the man who had come up to him where he was standing could be discerned as little more than a shadow.

'You are wanted,' the man said.

'Wanted?'

'By the President.'

'By President Cardona?' Payne could think of no reason why Cardona should wish to see him. Surely it could not be to discuss some new tactic for the defence of the palace; the time was long past for anything of that kind. Yet what else but military matters could there be to necessitate a meeting? He had never been on intimate terms with the man; it was hardly to be expected that anyone in his position would be; any contact that there had been between them had been strictly related to that business for which he had been recruited. Socially he and the President had had no contact, had moved in different circles. Yet now in this hour of crisis he was being summoned to the great man's presence. Why?

Well, there was one way of finding out.

'Where is he?'

'Come,' the messenger said. 'I will take you to him.'

They descended from the observation post on the outer wall from which Payne, with no small danger to himself, had been surveying the siege artillery when the light had been better and crossed the open ground between it and the palace building. This vast paved forecourt with its ornamental trees, its statuary, its formal beds of flowers and ornate fountains had become crammed with the implements of war. There were tanks and guns and army lorries which had retreated into this last pocket of resistance, churning up the gardens and damaging the statues. Tents had been set up to accommodate the soldiers and three of the tanks were stationed just inside the massive wrought iron gates to resist any attempt by the besiegers to force an entrance at that point. Yet nothing that the defenders might do could achieve anything more than a brief postponement of the moment when the gates would be broken open, the tanks destroyed and the palace itself overrun by the horde that was for the present camped outside its walls.

Payne could imagine what it would be like: the looting and the slaughter, for there would be no controlling the savagery of armed men eager to settle old scores. It would be a shambles and he would be caught up in it.

He and the man who had come for him made their way through the clutter of men and machinery, the human and non-human detritus of a bloody civil war, avoiding the shell-holes, until they came to the broad terraces leading up to the front entrance of the building.

Inside the palace Payne could sense a feeling of resignation; little groups of men in uniform were gathered here and there talking in low voices, and the very droop of their shoulders seemed to indicate an awareness of the hopelessness of the situation. There was no laughter, scarcely a smile even; these were men who had thrown in their lot with Cardona and had done well for themselves when the going had been good, but now that things had turned sour they could see no way out. Their gloomy features portrayed their feelings only too well, but Payne felt no sympathy for them; he was in as much peril as they, and the outlook for him was no less bleak than theirs.

His guide, a young lieutenant, whose uniform showed none of the stains of an active campaign but still retained that pressed and spotless condition which was the hallmark of a member of the President's staff, led the way to a lift which carried them down to a room in the basement where, reasonably safe from the bombing and shelling to which the palace was being subjected, the President and his military aides had retreated to make what plans they could.

There were at this time in fact no more than three high-ranking officers with Cardona, who was as usual dressed in his general's uniform, and Payne was introduced without ceremony. His entrance was acknowledged by a curt nod from the President and the lieutenant was dismissed with a gesture of the hand.

Cardona was a man of about fifty. He might once have been handsome, but self-indulgence had taken its toll; he had become grossly fat; there were pouches under his eyes, his face was mottled and the collar of his shirt was overwhelmed by the heavy folds of flesh beneath his chin. Yet he was still vain enough concerning his personal appearance to wear a wig in place of the natural hair which had beaten a retreat from the surface of his head. His voice was a deep bass.

'Come here, Payne,' he said, when the lieutenant had left the room.

Payne walked towards the end of a long table where the officers were seated in a little group. They all gazed at him as he approached and he was aware of a certain hostility in their eyes. Only Cardona looked at him with any evidence of favour.

Cardona indicated a chair and invited—or rather ordered—him to be seated. He sat down with one of the officers on his right and the other two facing him across the table. The President himself was seated at the end. But for the uniforms it would have had the appearance of a board meeting of which he was chairman.

'You will, of course, be wondering why I have sent for you,' Cardona said. 'Perhaps you are thinking that I wish to consult you on some military matter, some last minute plan to turn the tide of this conflict and snatch victory from the jaws of defeat.' He gave a harsh bitter laugh. 'That would require a miracle, and miracles no longer occur; if they ever did, which I doubt. No; we are doomed. You know that, don't you?'

Payne shrugged but said nothing.

'Of course you do. You are not a fool. If you were I would have no use for you. So you know as well as I do that this struggle is lost. Tomorrow or the next day or the day after that our defences will be overrun. This palace will be sacked; the men will be slaughtered and the women raped. It is the normal outcome of battles such as this.'

Why is he telling me all this? Payne wondered. He knows I know it perfectly well, and yet he has to spell it out. It was as though the man were revelling in this preview of the disaster so soon to overtake him and those around him. He did not mention the possibility of surrender, of an appeal for terms. Perhaps he realised that there would be no terms for him, unless it were a choice between the firing squad and the rope.

At least he had no family to worry about.

His wife was dead and the women he had were to him no more than playthings, taken to satisfy his lust. Payne believed there had been a daughter, but he had never seen her and did not think she was in the palace. Which was lucky for her.

'So,' Cardona said, 'let us rule out the miracles and get down to reality. I have sent for you because I believe you are a man I can trust; an honest man who will keep a bargain. Am I right?'

Payne shrugged again. 'What is my word worth on that? If the answer were no, would I say so?'

'Possibly not. So I have to depend on my own judgement. There are some with me here who would say I am mistaken. Is it not so, Bernardo?'

Colonel Bernardo Diaz was one of those sitting opposite Payne. He was a lean hollow-cheeked man in his early forties. There was a cadaverous look about him, a veritable Cassius, and maybe as dangerous.

'I think there are those amongst us who are at least equally as trustworthy. So why choose this man, a soldier of fortune, a foreigner and a mercenary?'

'Even a mercenary may be trusted to earn his pay. And there have, I believe, been honourable men who were born in other countries than this. Just as there are those born here whom I would not care to have behind my back. Some of them among my own closest allies perhaps.' He was looking hard at Diaz as he spoke and the implication was unmistakable.

Diaz's face darkened. 'That sounds like an accusation of disloyalty. Whom do you accuse?'

'No one. I was simply making an observation.'

'It seemed to be rather more than that.'

'Well, you must take it as you will. At a time like this every man should look into his own heart and ask himself where his allegiance lies.'

The other two officers had said nothing. They were also colonels and they seemed uneasy. In the circumstances that was hardly to be wondered at. One of them, Rafael Espinosa, was a small delicate-looking man, still quite young, with sleek black hair and a small moustache. The other, Tomas Salazar, was older, grizzled, heavy-jowled, with a nose that would have qualified him to play the part of Cyrano de Bergerac. He looked tired.

There was a brief silence in the room, finally broken by Cardona.

'Let us waste no more time. I have made my decision.' He spoke to Payne. 'I have an important assignment for you. You are to be my courier.'

'Courier!' It sounded crazy. At a time like this what need would he have of a courier? He could not be sending for reinforcements; there were none. He himself had admitted that all was lost.

'Yes,' Cardona said. 'You will be taking a small package to England.'

It became even more crazy. How was he to take anything to England? How was he to get there himself? How was he to leave the palace with the besiegers almost at the gates?

Cardona appeared to read his thoughts. 'You are wondering how you will get away from here? Perhaps you think it is impossible? It is not, though it will certainly be difficult. It will take courage and resourcefulness. I believe you have those qualities.'

'It is madness,' Diaz said. 'He will never make it. He will be caught and the thing will be taken from him.'

'That is a possibility, of course. But even if it happens nothing will be lost that would not have been lost anyway. Do you imagine those people out there hammering at the door will not take everything when the time comes?'

'Nevertheless—'

'Nevertheless,' Cardona broke in sharply, 'it will be done as I propose. I wish for no more argument.' He turned once more to Payne. 'You accept the commission?'

Payne did not hesitate. He had only the haziest idea of what he was being asked to do, but the salient feature of it was that he would escape the final carnage when the palace fell. He was being offered a way out; a dangerous and difficult way, no doubt, but at least a way. He would have been crazy to refuse.

'I accept it.'

'Good.'

'Did you doubt that I would?'

'No,' Cardona said, 'I had no doubt. After all, it is to your advantage. It is a way of escape, is it not? If you are successful you will be alive and you will be free. Whereas if you remain here—who knows?' A lift of the shoulders expressed it all. 'And now to business.'

He raised his great weight from the chair, lumbered over to a safe in the wall on his right, dialled the combination, opened it and took out a black metal cash-box, which he brought to the table. He sat down and unlocked the cash-box with a key from his pocket. When he raised the lid a bag made of blue velvet was revealed. He took it out, untied the string and opened the bag. He reached inside and drew out a small, round, many-faceted object which he held up between the thumb and forefinger of his right hand. Under the electric light it sparkled with an intense brilliance.

'Do you know what this is?' he asked.

The question was addressed to Payne and he answered it. 'I imagine it is a diamond.'

'And you are right. But it is no ordinary diamond. Once it adorned an Indian rajah's turban. How it came into my possession is a long story and I will not bore you with it.'

'It might not be so boring,' Payne said. He

could guess that the stone had not been acquired by any honest means. Theft had probably entered into the process; the jewel might have had a sorry tale to tell of murder and violence and all manner of chicanery if it could have spoken. A long story perhaps, but far from boring if the truth were told. But Cardona had no intention of telling it. The important point was that the diamond was in his hands now, and how it had come there was of no concern to him.

'What would you say a stone like this would be worth?'

Payne shook his head. 'It's out of my line. I'm no expert on the price of jewels.'

'Make a guess. It is a large stone, as you can see. And flawless.'

Cardona was speaking the truth. The stone was not a Cullinan or a Koh-i-Noor, but it was big nevertheless. Payne had no idea of its worth, but he plucked a figure out of the air.

'Fifty thousand.'

'Pesos, Deutsche marks, pounds sterling or American dollars?'

'Dollars.'

Cardona gave a contemptuous laugh. 'Multiply that by ten and you would still be far below the correct figure. Stones of this size and quality are rare, believe me.'

'I believe you,' Payne said. 'But what is all this to me?'

'It is much to you, my friend. You are going

to take this diamond to England and give it to my daughter.'

Payne stared at him. It was so unexpected. When Cardona had told him that he was to go to England on a mission he had imagined it would be a matter of delivering some kind of political communication, though he could not guess what. But now it appeared that the purpose of his journey was of a far more personal nature. Cardona, knowing that the end for him was near, must have decided to make this last gift to his daughter. And what a gift!

'So your daughter is in England?'

'Yes. At least, I assume she is. I have not heard from Maria in two years.'

'That is a long time.'

'It is. There was a misunderstanding between us. It does not matter now. And she is my only child. One remembers things of that sort at a time like this.'

Payne gathered that Cardona had decided to make this last gesture of conciliation with his daughter before he died. And indeed it would be a grand gesture, in keeping with the flamboyant character of the man.

Colonel Diaz was unable to remain silent any longer. 'This is crazy. You are throwing the stone away. This man will take it but he will not deliver it. He is, as I have said, a soldier of fortune and you are proposing to trust him with a fortune. It is too much to expect that he will not seize it for himself.'

Cardona looked at Payne. 'What do you say to that?'

'I say that the colonel has good reason for his doubts. But again I can only give you my word that I am honest. If you entrust me with this mission I promise that I will do my utmost to deliver the jewel to your daughter.'

'You would be prepared to swear an oath to that effect? On the Bible?'

'No.'

Cardona's eyebrows went up. He seemed taken aback by the answer. 'Why not?'

'Because it would be meaningless; no more binding than my plain word. I am not a religious man. It would be no more than a sham.'

'A man without principles,' Diaz sneered. 'A fine one to put so much trust in.'

'I did not say I was without principles,' Payne corrected him.

'But you are an atheist?'

'Perhaps. But because a man does not believe in God it does not necessarily follow that he is a thief and a cheat.'

Cardona slapped the table with his hand. 'Let us have an end of this. My mind is made up. I have chosen my courier and that is that.' He put the diamond back in the bag and passed a slip of paper across the table to Payne. 'That is the address in London where Maria was living when she last wrote to me. Whether she is still there I cannot say. You may have to make a search.'

Payne took the slip of paper, glanced at it and put it in his pocket.

'You will need money,' Cardona said. He turned to Colonel Salazar who held the post of paymaster general. 'Give him what was agreed.'

Salazar opened a briefcase that was lying on the table in front of him and extracted from it some bundles of paper money, which he handed to Payne. They were crisp and new, not pesos but American dollars, high value bills. There were also travellers cheques.

'Forty thousand dollars in all,' Cardona said. 'For expenses and payment for your services. Do you find that satisfactory?'

'It is generous,' Payne said. But of course Cardona could afford to be generous. What use would money be to him now?

'You may count it if you wish.'

'I'll take your word,' Payne said. 'When do I leave?'

'Tonight. There is no point in delaying matters.'

He was right about that, Payne thought. There was no telling how many more days the defences would hold out.

CHAPTER TWO

ENCOUNTER

He left the palace some time after midnight. He had shed the uniform that would have marked him out as a member of the government forces and was wearing a pair of blue jeans and a zipper-fastened gaberdine jacket. On his feet were soft leather shoes with rubber soles, and his head was bare except for the thatch of dark wiry hair which had been closely trimmed only a few days earlier.

The travellers cheques and dollars were in a money belt that encircled his waist next to the skin, and the diamond was in there too, the velvet bag having been discarded. For personal luggage he was carrying a small canvas duffel bag with a shoulder strap for ease of transport. He had two weapons with him: one was a hammerless revolver of .38 calibre with a two-inch barrel, a handy gun for the pocket and made by the American firm of Smith and Wesson; the other was a flick-knife, which had the advantage over the gun of being silent in use.

He was leaving as it were by the back door. The palace had been built close to the river, so close in fact that the rear wall rose sheer from the water and formed an artificial cliff past which the current glided on its way to the sea. The river was thus a part of the fortification, and though the enemy was established on the opposite bank and had launched one waterborne attack in open boats, the venture had been easily repulsed by the defenders and had not been repeated.

Payne had been conducted to a part of the building where he had never previously been. A last flight of stone steps led down to a narrow concrete basin, rectangular in shape, into which the river water came through a heavy iron grating, rather like a portcullis, which could be raised and lowered by a hand-operated winch. In the basin were a number of boats of various sizes, one of which was a small canoe. It was this canoe that was to be the means by which he would escape from the palace, relying on the darkness to hide him from any watchers who might be stationed on the opposite bank.

There were two men with him, and when they had helped him into the canoe one of them stationed himself at the winch and the other switched off the light. At first he could see nothing, but as his eyes became accustomed to the gloom he could just make out a slightly lesser darkness where the exit was. He heard the harsh sound of the grating being raised by the man at the winch, and a moment or two later the sound ceased and he knew that the way out was no longer barred.

The man who had switched off the light had returned to the edge of the concrete side of the basin and was leaning over the canoe. He uttered a gruff word or two of encouragement and then gave the canoe a shove with his hand. It floated towards the opening and with help from the paddle which Payne had taken in his hands emerged from its shelter into the open air. The current caught it and it began to move downstream like a piece of flotsam, the stars shining brilliantly overhead and a few lights visible on the opposite bank.

He used the paddle to bring the canoe into mid-stream, his object being to go down-river until he came to the port area where among the wharves and docks he hoped to be able to slip ashore unobserved and lose himself in the maze of old streets and buildings which clustered round this commercial gateway to the Caribbean Sea. Further ahead than that he had no firm plan; he would play it by ear and take things as they came.

The first thing that came was trouble. He had left the palace well behind and had come round a bend of the river when he heard the sound of a motor-boat engine. It was some distance ahead of him and was coming in his direction; he could see the lights on it and he dug his paddle in on the left side to alter the course of the canoe and drive it towards the right bank. But he had scarcely had time to make the manoeuvre when a spotlight was switched on in the bows of the motor-boat and he was caught in the beam. At the same time a voice, amplified by a loud-hailer, gave him a peremptory order to stop.

The fact that the order was worded in Spanish presented him with no difficulty in understanding it, since during his service in the army of President Cardona he had become well versed in that language. Nevertheless, he made no attempt to obey, but merely worked all the more vigorously with the paddle.

There were some ships lined up alongside the nearby quay and a wooden jetty thrust out a stubby finger into the river. It was towards this that he was heading, but the current threatened to sweep him past it and he had to fight with the paddle to keep the prow of the canoe pointing in the right direction.

He could hear the motor-boat coming up fast, and then a machine-gun began to chatter and bullets were zipping into the water all around and kicking up little bursts of spray. A few of them thudded into the woodwork of the canoe and it needed no more than this to convince Payne that it was not the safest spot for him and he had better move out quickly before one of those viciously whining bits of metal found its mark in his body. He took a deep breath, rolled himself over the gunwale of the canoe and slid beneath the surface. It had been necessary to abandon his duffel-bag, but it was a life and death matter and the bag had to go.

He swam underwater until his lungs were bursting and he had to come up for air. He was afraid that when he did so he might find himself in the white glare of the spotlight, but he was relieved to discover that the light was still directed at the canoe and that bursts of machine-gun fire were still being wasted on it. He could only guess that his dive overboard had not been observed and that the men in the motor-boat had mistaken the duffel-bag for its owner.

But the boat was getting very near to the canoe and it would not be long before the error was discovered and the search was turned on him again. He caught a glimpse of the jetty looming up in the darkness and he swam in that direction, hampered by his clothes but making good progress. In a minute or two he had his hand on one of the massive timber piles at the outward end of the structure, but he could hear men's voices, and turning his head he saw the motor-boat not more than thirty yards away.

There was no firing now, but one of the men had pulled the canoe up to the side with a boat-hook and they must have been able to see that all it had in it was his duffel-bag. He hoped they would conclude that he had been hit by a bullet and had fallen overboard and was dead. They might then go away and not bother him any more.

But of course it was too much to hope for, and a moment later the searchlight was beginning to sweep the water again. The beam was coming his way and he had to take another dive, and he was not sure even then that he had not been seen. When he came up for air the light was not shining on the jetty, but the boat had not gone away and the men in it had not abandoned the hunt. The engine was throttled back and the boat was moving at a slow pace close in to the shore, the light probing into every nook and cranny as it came towards the place where he was clinging to the jetty.

He slipped under the horizontal timbers and came up inside the framework, hanging there as the boat approached. The beam of light played on his hiding-place, but he had positioned himself behind one of the massive piles so that he was hidden from the searchers. It was apparent, however, that they suspected he might be there; he could hear them talking to one another, and then there was a bump as the boat came into contact with the end of the jetty and the propeller stopped turning.

It was so close to him now that he could have reached out with his hand and touched the hull. The searchlight had been switched off and he heard someone climbing up on to the jetty above his head; there were two of them and they had torches. They began walking along the jetty and shining the torches down on to the water, one on each side. Then they came back and halted just above the place where he was waiting, and someone in the boat called up to them, asking if they had found anything. One of the searchers answered sourly that they had not, and the man in the boat told them to come back on board.

He heard them scrambling down from the jetty, and the boat rocked as they stepped into it, sending little ripples of water in under the structure. Then it moved off a little way, but the propeller was still not turning, and all at once the searchlight came on again and a submachine-gun began to chatter. They were making sure there was nothing living under the jetty before going away and the bullets were kicking up spurts of water on each side of him. There were some slamming into the timber to which he was clinging and even chipping splinters of wood off the edges; and it was not just the chill of the water that was sending shivers down his spine now; it was also the feeling that at any moment one of those bits of metal might take a chip off him too.

But suddenly the firing stopped and he heard the engine revving up and knew that the hunters were leaving. With the searchlight gone it was dark under the jetty and there was a stench of weed and mud and general rottenness. It was time to be moving on.

There were steps at the end of the jetty, and he hauled himself on to them and climbed to the top. He was standing now where the two men had stood a little earlier, but unlike them he was sopping wet from head to foot and water was dribbling from him like rain from a gutter. He could still hear the motor-boat in the distance, but it seemed to be going away and he guessed that the men in it had either assumed that he was dead or had decided that he was not worth bothering about any more. So good riddance to them, he thought; they had done enough damage as it was, and he was resentful about losing his kit at the very outset of his journey. It was hardly a propitious beginning.

Looking round he could see the dark outlines of ships with lights showing here and there. But even on the nearest of these there was no sign of any life, though he would have thought the firing might have roused some interest. Still, in the state of things prevailing at the present time gunfire had become so much a part of everyday life that the odd machine-gun cracking away in the night would hardly be enough to bring anyone running. It would be more likely to persuade them to keep their heads down. Besides which, he had heard that a curfew had been imposed in the town, and this would apply to the dock area also.

He turned his back on the river and began to walk at a brisk pace along the jetty, shoes squelching and trousers clinging. At the landward end of it was a roadway and transit sheds and cranes, but all was dead and silent, and he hoped it would remain that way because the last thing he wanted was to walk into a military patrol or maybe some armed police who had thrown in their lot with the revolutionaries. He doubted whether it would be possible to find anyone in the town willing to confess openly that he was a supporter of President Cardona. Loyalty to a fallen dictator was apt to be pretty thin on the ground.

There were not many lights around the docks and he stayed in the shadows as much as possible, keeping a weather eye open for anyone else on the move, who was unlikely to be a friend and might well turn out to be an enemy. He had progressed some distance in this way and was beginning to think his luck was in when he heard a shout behind him.

'Stop!'

He swung round and saw two men dressed in a kind of uniform with berets on their heads and semi-automatic rifles in their hands. Men of the Army of Liberation, as it called itself, for a certainty, out and about to enforce the curfew. They were about fifty yards away and he guessed they had come out of a doorway or side-turning after he had gone past. He made a rapid mental assessment of the situation and came to the conclusion that there were only two alternative courses of action open to him: he could give himself up or he could make a run for it. If he gave himself up he would almost certainly be taken somewhere for questioning;

he would be searched and the diamond and the money would be found, and he could see no way of talking himself out of that kind of fix. On the other hand, if he made a run for it the men would without doubt shoot him in the back.

It took him just two seconds to reach a decision. He turned and ran.

He had gone maybe a dozen paces when they started firing.

He began to zigzag, hoping to throw them off their aim, and he could hear some of the bullets hitting the concrete and bouncing off with a thin whining sound like the cry of a banshee in the night.

By his own reckoning he had just one advantage: the men could either shoot him or run after him, but they could not effectively do both at the same time. He hoped they would give chase, because however bad they might be in the shooting line there was no telling when they might plant a lucky one plumb in the middle of his back, and a bullet from one of those rifles could go clean through you and do considerable damage on the way. He wanted none of that.

So it was with a feeling of relief that he heard no more firing, and glancing over his shoulder he saw that the men were running, carrying their rifles at the short trail. He had by now established a lead of nearly a hundred yards, but sodden trousers were a severe handicap to a running man and he was not at all sure he could outpace his pursuers. Another backward glance revealed the fact that they were indeed gaining on him, one some distance in front of the other.

At this rate he would soon be overtaken, or the leading man might be close enough to take another shot and maybe hit his target. He looked desperately for a way of escape, and suddenly one presented itself; the big sliding door of one of the sheds on his left was closed but there was a wicket in it which appeared to be slightly ajar. He altered course towards it and found that it had indeed been left unfastened; it swung inward under the weight of his hand and he plunged through the opening just as one of the rifles cracked again and a bullet smacked into the timber of the door.

It was dark inside, and still moving forward he came up against a stack of packing-cases. He moved away to the right and came to what appeared to be a passageway between two stacks. He went into this passage, finding his way more by touch than sight, and he heard the sound of his pursuers stepping into the shed. It seemed that they had come to a halt by the door and were conferring together; he could hear their voices and it was apparent that they were discussing the best way of running their quarry to earth.

They had the advantage; there were two of

them and it was probable that there was no other way out of the shed, so they had him cornered. He wondered whether after all it had been such a good idea to rush inside, but the decision had been taken on the spur of the moment and for good or bad he had to live with it now.

Suddenly lights came on in the roof of the shed. They must have found the switch, and now they would be coming to get him. Still, the light helped him to see where he was and he found that he was indeed in a corridor between two stacks of crates which reached almost to the girders of the roof. He had paused for a moment, listening to the men's voices, but now he got moving again and as soon as he came to a cross-passage he slipped into it. He heard another shout.

'Come on out! Come out with your hands up!'

He made no reply; it was probable that none had been expected. Then there was the crack of a rifle again, sounding much louder inside the building, and the screech of a ricochet off metal. But he knew it was just for show, a warning; they could not see him.

Nevertheless, they had time on their side; they had no need for haste. They would make a search and were bound to find him in the end. Unless he could double back to the door and make his escape. That was more easily said than done, but he had to try.

He came to a halt once more and gazed up at the stack of crates on his left. It was maybe ten or fifteen feet high, but there were plenty of handholds and footholds which would make it easy enough to climb. He had no sooner thought of this than he put it into practice, and a moment or two later he was stretched out flat on top of the upper crates.

It was not an instant too soon. He heard one of the hunters advancing down the passageway he had just left and he lay perfectly still, scarcely breathing as the man approached the spot. He hoped he was invisible from below but he could not be absolutely certain, and when the man came to a stop almost immediately below him he feared he had been detected. Suddenly he heard the man's voice.

'Come out of there! No use hiding. No place you can go from here. We have you cornered.'

Payne did not move. From what the man had said it was obvious to him that he had not been seen; the searcher was just hoping he would give himself up. But he had no intention of doing that. And then the man moved on again, muttering to himself.

Payne began to wriggle along the tops of the crates, moving diagonally in the direction of the doorway by which he had entered the building. If he could reach it while the men were searching elsewhere he might be able to slip out unnoticed and get clean away while they were still hunting for him inside.

But when he came to the edge of the stack and peered down he saw that he had been too hopeful and had underestimated the cunning of his adversaries. One of them was waiting by the wicket, obviously for the purpose of thwarting just such a move as he had had in mind. So it became necessary to think of something else, and the thing that came into his mind was the Smith and Wesson revolver. He reached into the pocket where it was and pulled it out. It had been immersed in water but he had no doubt that it was still in working order and he took careful aim. The man was not looking in his direction and he knew that a little pressure on the trigger would eliminate this obstacle once and for all.

Yet he hesitated to exert that pressure; to shoot the man in cold blood was not something that he cared to do, even though the man had undoubtedly shot at him and would certainly be prepared to do so again. There had to be another way. But what?

And then the man himself provided the answer. He moved a little closer to the stack of crates, leaned his rifle against it and took a cigarette from his pocket. He was quite young, scarcely more than a boy, but even boys were lethal when they had a Kalashnikov rifle in their hands, and this one might well have done his share of killing. He was just lighting the cigarette when Payne dropped on him.

It was a well-aimed drop. Payne's feet hit the

man's shoulders and knocked him to the floor. He had given a cry as he fell, but he did not even attempt to get up because Payne hit him with the revolver just in the right spot and put the snuffers on him.

The other man must have heard the cry and he put in an appearance just as Payne reached the wicket. He gave a yell and Payne turned and saw him. He was an older man than the one on the floor, with swarthy complexion and a thick moustache. He was about fifteen yards away and aiming the rifle. Payne dived forward as he pressed the trigger and the bullet missed him by a hair's-breadth. From the prone position he fired the revolver and got the man in the right shoulder. The man screamed and dropped the rifle.

Payne stepped out through the wicket and ran. No one came after him in pursuit.

CHAPTER THREE

DREAM

The house was not in one of the more select parts of the town, though it was some way from the dock area. It took Payne quite a while to reach it, and he had had two or three narrow escapes from falling foul of patrols of armed men who were evidently engaged in seeing that the curfew was not broken. But he got there at last and found the place in darkness, as was only to be expected at that hour of the night. It was several minutes before he could get any response to the bell, and he was beginning to think she was not at home, or had maybe even gone away altogether, when a light came on in an upstairs room and a little later he heard her voice on the other side of the door.

'Who is it? Who's there?'

She sounded nervous, a bit suspicious, as well she might. These were perilous times to be living in.

'It's me,' he said. 'Alan. Open up, Bel.'

He heard her sliding the bolts back and turning the key in the lock, and then the door opened just enough to let him in before she closed and locked and bolted it again.

'You certainly believe in making things safe,' he said.

'It's the sensible thing to do, isn't it? Not that a locked door would keep those pigs out if they really meant to get in. They would break it down.'

They were in a narrow hallway from which the stairs rose steeply, and there was only a small electric light bulb for illumination. The woman was in a dressing-gown and slippers, and her black hair was cascading over her shoulders.

'I wasn't expecting to see you,' she said. 'I heard they'd got you all bottled up in the palace and nobody could get out.'

'You heard correctly.'

'Then how—?'

'There's a way out. But it's not easy. I had trouble. I lost my kit and had to do some swimming.'

She seemed to notice his bedraggled condition for the first time. 'Oh, my God, you're wet through. You must take those clothes off at once. How did it happen?'

'I'll tell you, later. First I think it would be best if I had a bath.'

'Yes,' she said. 'Yes, do that.'

She followed him up the stairs; he knew the way, knew it well. His shoes still made a squelching sound but the water was no longer draining out of his clothes.

It was no great shakes as a bathroom; it would never have made the pages in a glossy women's magazine; but it was adequate. The woman set the bath-water running and took his wet clothes from him as he peeled them off. She said she would carry them down to the kitchen and hang them up to dry. The money-belt came off last, but that was one thing he did not let her take; he wanted to keep it near him. He was not worried that the contents might have got wet; it was made of waterproof material and the fastening sealed the pouches. In it, besides the money and the jewel, were his British passport and one or two other items. She was about to take it with the clothes, but he stopped her.

'I'll keep that with me.'

It caused her to raise her eyebrows. 'Why? Don't you trust me with it?'

'Of course I do. It's just that I feel happier having that where I can keep an eye on it.'

'Ah!' she said. 'So there's something important in there.'

'Yes. My passport.'

He knew that she did not believe it was the passport that was making him so careful with the money-belt, but she said nothing more. She went away with the clothes and he stepped into the bath.

He had been telling the truth when he had said that he trusted her. He did, up to a point. He felt certain she would never have robbed him, but he was not so certain that she would not have looked inside the money-belt just to satisfy her curiosity. And though she might not have taken the diamond he did not want her to know that it was there. The fewer people who knew about that, the better; and what she did not know she could not tell.

The belt was strapped round his waist when he came down from the bathroom, but it was not visible because he was wearing a dressing-gown. The gown and a pair of slippers on his feet belonged to him; they were kept in the house in readiness for whenever he might need them. He felt at home there, but he would soon be leaving perhaps for the last time. Soon he would have to tell her that, and it would not please her.

She was in the kitchen and there was a smell of coffee freshly made. His clothes were hanging up to dry but the revolver and the flick-knife were lying on the table.

'The gun has been fired,' she said.

'Yes, it has.'

'But only one bullet. Did you kill the man?'

'No. I think I hit him in the shoulder.'

'There was only one?'

'No, there were two. They had me cornered in a transit shed down by the docks. I jumped on the other one and knocked him out.'

'But before that you had to swim?'

'Yes. I was in a canoe, but a patrol boat caught me with a searchlight. I was lucky to escape. I had to hide under a jetty. They threw a lot of lead in my direction, but somebody must have been watching over me; I could have ended floating down the river to the sharks in the Caribbean.'

'Oh, God!' She shivered as if suddenly cold, and she looked concerned. 'Will they be hunting for you?'

'They'll be hunting for somebody. I don't see how they could know it's me. Unless the man I shot recognised me. But that's unlikely; I'm not that well known.'

'I don't know.' She sounded doubtful. 'It's not as if you're just any government soldier. You're the man who trained the Palace Guard.

They'll want to get you.'

She could have been right at that, Payne thought. Maybe the new lot in power would regard him as a criminal. It was possible. He had better see to it that he was not picked up.

She poured the coffee. Her name was Isabel Romero and she was a cabaret singer. She was about thirty and seductively attractive with that silky black hair and those big dark eyes and generous mouth that might have been made just for kissing.

The cabaret was not one of the classier establishments of its kind and she was not earning a hell of a lot. He had been introduced by another of the President's men and had liked the look of her from the start. She seemed to take to him too, and soon they were lovers. The affair had been going on for nearly a year now and neither of them had grown tired of the other. He had asked her once whether she had any thoughts of making it to the big time, maybe in the States; Las Vegas perhaps.

'Big money there, so I've heard.'

She had laughed. 'Sure, I've thought of it. Who wouldn't in my situation? But you have to be realistic about these things. I'm not so young any more and my talent is limited. I just haven't got what it takes.'

'I think you underrate yourself.'

'Don't flatter me, Alan. You know I'm not terribly good.'

'For my money you're the tops.'

But he knew she was right. She was not going anywhere. She had probably reached the summit of her career and from here on in it would all be downhill. Not the rosiest of prospects.

And now he was going to leave her. That was for certain.

'What are you going to do?' she asked, as though reading his mind.

'I have to get away,' he said. 'Out of the country.'

She seemed to wince, and her eyes clouded like a sky suddenly overcast. 'So you are leaving me?'

'It's necessary. For a time.'

'But can you do that? Won't they be checking at the ports and the airport and all the border posts?'

'It's pretty certain that they will.'

'Then how will you manage it?'

'I don't know. Maybe I can slip across into Mexico and take it from there.'

'It would be difficult, wouldn't it?'

'Probably.'

She drank some coffee and thought about it.

'Does Cardona know you have left the palace?'

Payne smiled. 'It would be hard for anyone to leave without his knowledge.'

'And you had his permission?'

'He certainly raised no objection.'

She gave him a shrewd look. 'I think he sent

you.'

'Now why would he do that?'

'Perhaps he needed a courier and you were the one chosen for the task. Am I right?'

'Please,' he said, 'don't ask questions.'

Suddenly she seemed to think of something. 'Of course. That money-belt. It's in there, isn't it?'

'What is?'

'This letter, dispatch, whatever it is you have to deliver. That's why you refused to let the belt out of your sight.'

'You're just guessing. Forget it.'

'Very well then, if you don't want to tell me you don't have to. But you really are in trouble, aren't you? I think you need help.'

'Frankly,' he said, 'I need all the help that's going, but I can't see where any is coming from. This is something I have to do on my own.'

Again she appeared to do some thinking. Then:

'Perhaps I could help.'

'You? What could you do?'

'I know some people who might get you out. It would cost money. Have you any?'

'I have some. But these people; who are they? How could they manage it?'

'Never mind who they are. Not for the present. I shall have to contact them and sound them out. Do you want me to go ahead?'

He was doubtful. He was not sure he liked

the sound of it. What kind of people could they be who would be willing to help a fugitive get out of the country? Could he trust them? From what she had said it sounded as if they were going to be bribed, and characters who took bribes were inclined to be the dodgy kind who would double-cross you at the drop of a hat.

'I'm not sure,' he said. 'It sounds risky. I'd be putting myself in their hands.'

'It wouldn't do any harm to meet them and hear what they have to say. You don't have to tell them why you want to get away or even who you are if you don't want to. If you don't like the look of them you don't need to go through with it.'

There seemed to be some logic in that, and he finally agreed to her suggestion. She said she would arrange the meeting but it might not be for a day or two. Meanwhile, he could stay at her place. With luck no one would come looking for him there.

* * *

He ventured out the next day. He had to buy some kit to replace what he had lost in the river. He wore a pair of dark glasses and hoped that he would not be recognised by anyone. He bought the minimum of clothing and toilet gear and a canvas holdall to carry it in. Now and then he heard the sound of gunfire coming from the other side of the river where the siege of the President's Palace was still going on, but in the town life seemed almost back to normal. Here and there damaged buildings gave evidence of the street-fighting that had taken place; but that was all finished now, though there were still plenty of armed men moving around, some on foot, some in troop-carriers; and there were tanks stationed under trees and in the plazas, grimly menacing.

It was hot and he had left the zipper jacket in the house with the gun and the knife, just wearing an open-necked shirt and the jeans which Isabel had ironed. The shoes had still been damp when he had put them on, but they had dried quickly in the sun and there was nothing in his appearance to make him at all conspicuous.

He had completed his shopping and was about to return to the house when he had a shock. He was standing on the pavement, bag in hand, waiting to cross one of the main streets, when a car went by; a big grey Mercedes driven by a swarthy man in a peaked chauffeur's cap. But it was not the driver who caught Payne's attention; it was one of the two men sitting in the back, a man who looked remarkably like Colonel Bernardo Diaz. The other was dressed in the uniform of an officer of the revolutionary army, but Diaz, if it was he, was wearing a white civilian suit and a Panama hat. He was talking to the man at his side and did not glance in Payne's direction. A moment later the car had gone past and was hidden from sight by the other traffic.

When he got back to the house Isabel was preparing lunch. He told her what he had seen.

'You are certain it was Colonel Diaz?'

'Practically certain.'

'If you only saw him going past in a car it may simply have been someone who looked like him. I mean you must have had no more than a passing glimpse of him.'

'That's true. But I'm still convinced it was him.'

'But what would he have been doing, riding with an enemy officer?'

'That's what I'd like to know. There's a smell of treachery here. I just wonder how long he may have been a traitor in the President's camp and how much he may have aided the other side. A man like him, privy to all Cardona's strategy, even helping to plan that strategy, would have been tremendously valuable to the revolutionary high command. And now, of course, with the thing practically all over, he slips away, joins up with the people he's been selling out to and gets driven around in a smart German car. No need for him to stick around for the final slaughter which he might get caught up in; clear out and save his own skin while the rest of them perish. What a bastard!'

'But this is all conjecture. You don't even know for certain it was him you saw.'

'I'd make a bet it was.' And then a thought

came into his head which, oddly enough, had not occurred to him before. It was almost as much of a shock as that first sight of the man in the car. 'He could be looking for me.'

'Why would he be doing that?'

'Because he knows what errand I'm on. He was there when I was given the assignment. He wasn't in favour of it. He argued against Cardona entrusting me with it, but he was overruled. He knows what I'm carrying.'

'Which is more than I do,' Isabel said, a trifle tartly.

He hardly seemed to hear her. For another thought had come into his head. 'Of course! He wants it for himself.' He remembered the glitter in Diaz's eyes when Cardona produced the diamond. He had thought little of it at the time, but now he had no doubt that it had been an indication of the man's burning desire; he wanted the jewel so much that it had perhaps been almost impossible for him not to stretch out his hand and grasp it there and then. That was why he had so strongly objected to Cardona's entrusting it to Payne; he could not bear to think of its being carried beyond his reach. Maybe he had already been planning to snatch it when the palace fell.

'What does he want for himself?' Isabel asked.

'Never mind.'

'So you're still not going to tell me?'

'It would only worry you.'

'You think it doesn't worry me not knowing?'

She was still working at the cabaret, but the hours had changed. It was opening earlier in the day because the imposition of the curfew meant that it could not be kept open so late. She had to hurry home after her last appearance to make sure she was not caught by a patrol on the streets after hours.

Politically she was neutral; she bore allegiance to neither side in the struggle for power, but if anything she would have preferred the *status quo* because she feared the left-wing revolutionaries would be more puritanical and might clamp down on the night life of the town even after the curfew had been lifted; which would be bad for entertainers like her.

'I'll tell you one day,' Payne said.
'And when will that be?'
'When I come back.'

She gave a sad little shake of the head. 'You will never come back. It would not be safe for you with the new regime in power. They will remember how you helped Cardona. When you go away it will be for ever. You know that, don't you?'

He did know it. They had had some good times together, but now they were approaching the end of the affair. He was sorry about that; it would be a wrench and he would feel the loss. But perhaps not as much as she would; perhaps it was always easier for the one who was going away. And he would have no time for brooding; there would be too much else to do. If he managed to get away.

'Perhaps things will change,' he said. 'This lot may not stay in power. Then I could come back. Or you might come to me.'

'To England?'

'Yes. Why not?'

'Because—' She gave an expressive shrug. 'It's a nice dream, but you know it will never happen.'

'It could,' he said. But he knew there was no conviction in the words. As she had said it was just a dream.

CHAPTER FOUR

ASSET

It was two days later when the meeting took place. There were two of them and they came to the house. The man had ginger hair and an unkempt beard; he was about thirty and chunky. He had blue eyes and freckles and a snub nose. His name was George Kay.

The woman was maybe a little younger, but she had a weathered look; exposure to the sun and the wind and salt spray had done no good at all to her skin. She was a blonde, hair all over the place; not bad-looking, not good either, just ordinary; figure more sturdy than sylphlike. She answered to the name of Diana Penny.

They were both a bit down-at-heel, and Payne was not favourably impressed by their appearance. An American might have taken one look at them and put them down as bums.

'So you're English,' Payne said.

The man gave a crooked sort of grin. 'Does it bother you?'

'No, it doesn't bother me. It's just that I didn't know.'

With a kind of perversity Isabel had told him nothing about them. He had not even known that one of them would be a woman. He had doubts at once as to whether they could help him; the meeting looked like being a total waste of time.

'Well, now you do know,' Kay said. 'I understand you want to get out of this damned country.'

'That's so.'

'So do we.'

They were sitting round the kitchen table. Isabel had made coffee and brought out a tin of biscuits. The man and the woman were eating their way through the biscuits as though they had not had a square meal in months.

'You want to get out?' Payne said. 'So what's preventing you?'

'Just what prevents all sorts of people doing

all sorts of things in this sad old world—a lack of the wherewithal, the spondulicks, the jolly old folding money. In a word, we're skint.'

'You mean you have nothing?'

'Not a cent.'

Payne glanced at Isabel, and the glance asked the question: 'Why in hell have you brought these people here?'

She seemed unconcerned. She spoke to Kay. 'You have an asset, though. Tell him what it is.'

'Ah, yes,' Kay said. 'The asset.' He looked at Payne. 'We have a boat.'

'Aha!' Payne thought about it. Then: 'What kind of boat?'

'Sailing. A small yacht, I suppose you might call it.'

'I see. And why, if you have this boat, can't you leave the country any time you feel like it?'

'As I told you, it's a question of money. We owe harbour dues and other things, and we're clean out of provisions.'

Payne was beginning to get the picture. 'So I'm to pay your debts and restock the larder for you in exchange for a passage to where I want to go?'

'Plus a fee for transport. Where do you want to go?'

'Jamaica will do nicely.' He could get an airline flight from there to London. 'What would your price be all told?'

Kay took an old envelope and a stub of pencil from his pocket and jotted down some figures. He added them up, drew a line under the total and said: 'In round figures let's say two thousand American dollars.'

Payne whistled softly. 'That's a bit steep.'

Kay shrugged. 'You want to get away, don't you? I'm not asking you why and I'm not asking why you can't leave openly like any ordinary British citizen. The way I look at it, we could be doing something illegal in taking you. That's a risk we're prepared to accept, but it's worth something. Wouldn't you agree?'

'I could try some other way.'

'Sure you could; but do you know of a better one?'

Payne could see that Kay knew he had a good hand and intended playing it for all it was worth. Well, maybe that was fair enough. If the roles had been reversed he would probably have done the same.

'This boat of yours. I suppose it's seaworthy?'

It was the woman, Diana, who answered that one. 'You don't need to worry on that score. We sailed in her from England, didn't we? We've been all over the world in her. It's our life.'

'But now you're stranded.'

'Temporarily.'

'Well,' Payne said, thinking it over, 'it seems to me you need me as much as I need you. You're not likely to find another customer willing to bail you out of the fix you're in.

Right?'

Neither of them said anything; they just looked at him, poker-faced. They did not seem worried. He guessed they had been in scrapes before; they were water tramps, going from place to place, picking up what they could. The life had made them tough. But they were the sort of people he needed.

'One thousand dollars,' he said.

'You must be joking,' the woman said. She took a tin from her pocket, opened it and began to roll a cigarette with the dark stringy tobacco inside. She handed the cigarette to the man and rolled another for herself. She was good at it, very deft with her fingers; the cigarette had a limp appearance, but that was typical of the hand-rolled variety. The man lighted them with a match. The smoke had a rank odour, as though it were from old rope burning.

'Fifteen hundred,' he said.

'All right. Half now and the rest when we reach Jamaica.'

They were not happy about that; they would have preferred to have the lot in advance. But he was adamant; he had to have some hold over them. He noticed that they did not argue that the seven hundred and fifty would be insufficient to pay off what they owed and buy the necessary provisions, so he concluded that it was enough. With the extra money waiting for them on completion of the voyage he could be pretty sure they would do their damnedest to get him to his destination.

In the end they surrendered with good grace. Perhaps they had been prepared to settle for less and were well satisfied with what they were getting.

Kay grinned. 'You drive a hard bargain, Alan. But hell, why not? You look like a man after my own heart.' He turned to his companion. 'What do you say, Di?'

She took a pull at the cigarette and breathed out some of the acrid smoke, squinting at Payne through the drifting veil.

'He'll do.'

*   *   *

Payne went down to the harbour with Kay and Diana to look at the boat. He was wearing the dark glasses and a white cotton sun-hat pulled well down, but nobody seemed interested in him.

The marina was nearer the mouth of the river than that part where the merchant ships berthed to discharge their cargoes and take on board the products of the Republic: coffee, cotton, bananas, timber... Down at this end of the port the commercial buildings gave way to better-class residences and hotels for the tourists who in the good times were attracted by the tropical climate and the sandy beaches. For the present the tourist trade had been ruined by the civil war and there were very few boats in the marina. The international yachting brigade had pulled out pretty smartly when the fighting approached the capital and Cardona's regime looked like toppling. The plush hotels were practically empty too; people liked to feel safe when on holiday, and the package tours had been put temporarily on hold.

The name of the boat was *Vagabond*, and Payne thought it fitted. *Vagabond* was an old yacht and had that same rather down-at-heel and vagrant look that distinguished her owner and his girlfriend. There was no fibre-glass or plastic in her construction, no gleaming chromium plate, no rakish lines about the bows or superstructure. This craft had obviously been built when wood had still been the natural material for boats and moulded hulls had scarcely been thought of. Captain Slocum himself would not have felt out of his element in her.

'So,' Payne said, standing on the quay and surveying this elderly vessel from stem to stern before stepping on board, 'this is it. This is what I'm paying all that money for. Not very impressive, is she?'

'Well, what did you expect?' Kay was on the defensive. 'The royal yacht?'

Vagabond was not large, possibly thirty feet long and eight or nine in the beam. She was ketch rigged, having two masts and a short bowsprit. At present the sails were furled and the only movement the boat was making was a very limited one up and down, which made the fenders squeak faintly as they were squeezed between hull and quay. There was an iron chain looped round the mizzen-mast and passing through a stout ring on the shore. It was fastened with a heavy padlock.

'I see they're making sure you don't slip away without paying your dues,' Payne remarked.

'Bastards,' Kay said. 'I don't know that it's strictly legal under international law. But what can I do?'

'Nothing except pay up. I imagine they make their own laws here.'

An occasional rumble of gunfire from the direction of the President's Palace some way upriver and on the opposite bank gave evidence that the final struggle was still going on. From this distance there was a sense of unreality about it; but Payne knew only too well that it was real enough for those engaged in it.

'Let's go aboard,' Kay said. 'You'll be wanting to see your quarters.'

He led the way. The accommodation was limited and Spartan. You went down a few steps from the cockpit into a small saloon, one corner of which served as the chartroom and another as the galley. On each side of a central table were settees which doubled as bunks.

Forward of the saloon was the toilet space leading to two more berths, crammed in where the hull narrowed towards the bows.

'This is where you'll be,' Kay said. 'Diana and I'll sleep in the saloon. We'll be taking turn and turn at the helm when we're at sea, of course. Okay?'

'Okay,' Payne said.

He was not favourably impressed. Everything was cramped, worn, untidy; it was like nothing so much as a floating garret lived in by impecunious artists. But he was a soldier and had experienced worse conditions than this. And it would not be for long. Jamaica was only six or seven hundred miles away. Not that *Vagabond* looked the kind of yacht that would win any sailing races. Still, as long as she stayed afloat ... And as the woman had said, they had sailed all over the place in her, so she had to be seaworthy.

On the way back to the house he noticed that the shelling had stopped. From the direction of the President's Palace there was an ominous silence. He wondered whether it was finished, whether the last resistance had crumbled and the revolutionaries had moved in.

On the streets there seemed to be an air of expectancy, as though everyone were waiting for some announcement. Little groups of people had gathered and were talking animatedly. He avoided them and went on his way, taking a tram for part of the journey. In the tram the passengers seemed to have caught the general fever of anticipation. He heard a woman say quite loudly: 'They will kill Cardona. It is all over now.' Then she fell silent, as though shocked by her own statement.

Isabel was still in the house. She seemed relieved to see him.

'I was worried about you. You have heard the news?'

'What news?'

'It was on the radio. They've stormed the palace and the President is dead.'

'So they did kill him?'

'I don't know. There was nothing to say how he died. Perhaps he was executed.'

'I doubt it. They would have had a show trial first.'

'Maybe somebody shot him in the heat of the moment.'

'I'd say it's more likely he shot himself. He would have known it was all over for him.'

She spoke anxiously. 'Now you must get away. It is not safe for you here. When will the boat be ready to leave?'

'The day after tomorrow, I think. I've given George the money and he'll be seeing about paying everything and getting stores on board. It shouldn't take long. They're going to let me know as soon as they're ready.'

She pressed his hand. 'I'm so afraid for you. You had better not go out again until the time comes. You're safer here.'

There was some truth in that. And there was no need for him to go out again; he had all he needed for the voyage.

'Are you going to the cabaret tonight?'

'Yes. I must.'

'I thought perhaps, seeing that it's possibly our last night—'

'My darling,' she said, 'I should like to stay here with you; you must know that. But it would not be wise. It is better if I appear as usual. But I will come home as early as I can.'

He had to agree that she was right. It was best to act normally. But he would have liked to have her there with him. It was going to be a long and tedious evening.

* * *

Next day Diana Penny turned up to report that all formalities had been dealt with and the stores were on board.

'George says you had better join ship this evening after dark. What do you think?'

'I think he's right. I must try to slip aboard without being seen.'

'If you like I'll take your kit when I go back.'

'That would be a help.' He could move more freely if he was not burdened with the holdall. 'There's not a lot. I'll be travelling light.'

She gave him a sharp quizzing glance. 'Running away from something, are you?'

'Not exactly.'
'Uh-huh! Well, it's none of my business.'
She went away carrying the holdall.

* * *

'How did you get to know those two?' Payne asked.
'Oh, they used to come to the cabaret and we would talk,' Isabel said. 'They're good company. Happy-go-lucky.'
'What were they using for money?'
'They had some at first. When it ran out they would do jobs about the place for peanuts and the odd free meal. They've been living from hand to mouth.'
'I must have come as a godsend to them.'
'You needed them too. Don't forget that.'

* * *

He stayed in the house when she went off to work. He knew she would be back again before he left because of the curfew which was still in force for the present. He had had some difficulty in deciding whether to go to the boat before the curfew started or after. Earlier in the evening there would be public transport available and there would be people on the streets with whom to mingle; later he would have to do the whole journey on foot and would run the risk of being picked up by the police or an army patrol. There could be little doubt that the post-curfew alternative would be the more dangerous, yet he chose it because in the middle of the night there would be less chance of his being seen going aboard. There was, moreover, the fact that he would have a few more hours with Isabel before the last farewell.

She was later than usual in returning and he was beginning to worry about her when she walked in.

'What kept you?' he asked. 'I was afraid you might have been arrested for breaking the curfew.'

She explained that there had been more customers than usual at the cabaret. It seemed that there were a lot of people celebrating the end of the conflict. Many of them were members of the revolutionary army and they would not let her go until she had sung a number of encores.

'I began to think I would never get away. They didn't seem to give a damn about the curfew. They had drunk a lot and were having a good time. I suppose you can't blame them.'

'No, I don't blame them,' Payne said. 'But I'm glad you got here safely. I wouldn't have wanted to leave without even saying goodbye.'

It was a long and loving goodbye which lasted until the small-hours. It was getting on for two o'clock when he said he would have to go.

'I'll come with you,' she said. 'As far as the marina.'

He saw that she was already getting dressed, pulling on a pair of jeans. It was not in the programme as he had planned it. By his reckoning the parting was to have been in this house, but it was evident that she had other ideas.

'You can't,' he said. 'You'll only be putting yourself at risk to no purpose.'

She brushed the argument aside. 'There is a purpose. I was born in this city. I have lived here all my life. I know all the back streets and alleyways where the patrols are not likely to be. I'll show you the way. You'll be much safer with me for a guide.'

He saw that there was logic in this, but he was reluctant to allow her to take the risk. 'You'll be in double danger, because you'll have to make the journey both ways. I won't let you do it.'

'You can't stop me.'

It was the truth, and as she seemed quite determined to have her way he was obliged to give in. Before setting out she made some coffee and they each drank a cup.

'It may be the last we shall have together,' she said regretfully.

'Look on the bright side. There could be many more.'

'A dream, Alan. Only a dream.'

*   *   *

They drank the coffee quickly and left the house. The street outside was deserted and they set out at a rapid walking pace. Soon they were moving through the backwaters of the city, where Payne had never previously ventured. The lighting in these areas was poor and they flitted from shadow to shadow, their shoes making scarcely a sound. They met no one; the place was empty because of the curfew, except at one point where they stumbled over what appeared to be a dead body, but which on closer examination turned out to be a drunk sleeping it off and snoring.

They encountered only one patrol in this area, and they were able to avoid it by darting into a narrow alleyway. But they had to leave these parts eventually and come out into the more open residential district near which the marina was situated. And it was here they ran into trouble.

They were walking down a wide boulevard, tree-lined and with houses on each side fronted by well-kept lawns and gardens. Suddenly a jeep came out of a side-turning some fifty yards ahead and drove towards them. They turned and ran, the jeep coming up behind, accelerating. It would have overtaken them in no time at all if they had stayed on the boulevard, but providentially an escape route appeared on the left. It was a footpath between two properties, too narrow for a vehicle, and without hesitation they took this way and continued running.

Payne heard the jeep come to a halt at the entrance to the footpath and a man shouting to them to stop. They ignored the order and ran on. There was the sharp crack of a pistol and a bullet hummed past. But the footpath took a bend to the right and for the moment they were out of sight of the pursuit.

On one side was a tall chain-link wire fence enclosing what could have been tennis-courts, and then suddenly the path came out on to another road lighted by street-lamps but deserted and very quiet.

Payne felt Isabel's hand tugging at his sleeve. 'This way.'

He allowed himself to be guided by her, and they ran off to the left. But the road went straight on for about a hundred yards and they had not gone far before they were being shot at again. Payne glanced back and saw that there were two men giving chase. They were not carrying rifles, but each one had a pistol in his hand and they were firing as they ran. This kind of shooting had to be pretty wild, but there was no telling when a lucky shot might find its mark and Payne decided it would be a good idea to get off the road very smartly indeed.

This time it was he who led the way. There was a house fronting on to the road with a low wall enclosing a garden of shrubs and lawns.

With a word to Isabel to follow him he vaulted over the wall and ran across the grass to a path at the side of the house leading to the back. Here they came upon a patio and some steps down to another lawn and a garden which was in almost complete darkness. They were moving blindly now, brushing past small trees and bushes, trampling on soft earth and stumbling over obstructions.

They were brought to a sudden halt by a wooden fence. Behind them Payne could hear men's voices. Lights came on in the house. A door opened. Someone demanded angrily to be told what in hell was going on.

'Let's get out of this,' Payne said.

The fence was about six feet high. He helped Isabel to climb over it and followed quickly himself. On the other side was another footpath, dimly visible.

'Which way now?' she asked. She seemed to have lost her sense of direction.

There was no time for hesitation; the pursuers might have been checked for the moment but it would not be long before they were on the trail again. Payne made a quick decision and took the right hand way. A few seconds later they came out on to a tree-lined boulevard which seemed oddly familiar. He glanced to the left and there, some hundred yards away, was the parked Jeep.

'Jesus!' he said. 'We've been going round in a circle. Let's get away from here. It's not healthy.'

They began to run again, away from the jeep. Very shortly they were out of sight of it and there had been no sign of the pursuit. Five minutes later they had reached the marina and there was not a soul in sight.

They had decided already that Isabel should not accompany him to the yacht, and it was here in the shadow of a dark and silent timber building that they parted with a last hurried kiss.

'Take care of yourself, Alan.'

'You too, Bel. We'll meet again.'

'Oh, sure,' she said. And he knew she did not believe it. There was a catch in her voice and if there had been enough light he guessed he would have seen tears in her eyes.

'Thanks for everything, Bel.'

'It was good for me too. While it lasted.'

She turned and began to walk away, almost breaking into a run as if in a hurry to be gone now that the time had come. He watched her go, wondering whether she would look back; but she did not, and in another moment she had vanished into the gloom, walking swiftly, walking perhaps out of his life for ever.

CHAPTER FIVE

EMBARKATION

They were awake and waiting for him. They seemed relieved when he stepped on board.

'We were a bit worried about you,' Kay said. 'Did you have any trouble getting here?'

'A little.'

'Want to talk about it?'

'No.'

'Well, anyway, you're here now,' the woman said. 'That's the main thing. And tomorrow we'll be on our way.'

'Today actually,' Kay said. 'Until then you'd better stay below. I hope nobody saw you come aboard.'

'I didn't see anyone and I don't think there was a soul about. The place seemed dead.'

'It's been pretty quiet ever since the war came this way and nearly all the boats moved out. About the only ones left are those with local owners and ours.'

'Have you had any sleep?' Payne asked.

Kay shook his head. 'No. We've been playing cards to pass the time.'

The cards were lying on the table in the saloon, where the three of them were talking. Payne guessed that neither of the other two had felt like turning in until he was safely on board.

'Well,' he said, 'maybe we should all get some shuteye now. I suppose we'll be leaving in a few hours' time.'

Kay agreed that it would be a good idea, but before they could act on it there came a diversion. They all heard the sound of a motor vehicle coming to a halt; then men's voices.

'Now what's all that?' Diana asked. She sounded worried.

'I don't know,' Kay said. 'But I don't much like it. You two stay here and I'll go and take a look.'

He went out of the saloon but was back almost immediately, looking distinctly unhappy.

'There's a jeep and a couple of soldiers further along the quay. It looks as if they're starting to search the boats.' He glanced at Payne. 'Any chance they might be looking for you?'

Payne thought it possible. He wondered whether it was the same jeep and the same two men he had already encountered, though how could they have guessed he was heading for the marina? But even if it was a different jeep and different men he was in trouble just the same if they came on board. He cast a glance round the saloon and Kay appeared to read his mind.

'There's nowhere in here you can hide.'

He saw that this was true. Yet if he climbed up on to the quay and tried to get away the chances were that he would be spotted and caught. He racked his brains for a solution to the problem and could think of only one.

'I shall have to go over the side.'

Kay seemed about to raise objections but decided not to. 'Okay, but you'll need a rope to hang on to. I'll fix one in the bows.'

Payne lost no time in stripping off his jacket and discarding his shoes, and a few seconds later Kay was back in the doorway beckoning to him. He went up the steps to the cockpit and caught a glimpse of the jeep some fifty yards away on the quay. There was one man standing beside it with a rifle; the second man was evidently making a search of one of the other yachts.

'Quick now,' Kay said. 'He's not looking this way. Keep your nut down and don't make a splash.'

The stern of the yacht was below the level of the quay and Payne lowered himself into the water with scarcely a sound. Swimming close to the hull he made his way to the bows where he found the rope dangling. He grasped it and hung there with his head just above the surface. While he waited he had the opportunity to reflect that this was the second time within a few days that he had been obliged to hide himself in this river, and it was not an experience he had any wish to repeat. He just hoped the men would not keep him waiting long.

In fact he had very little time to wait. He had

not been in the water for more than ten minutes when he heard the jeep approaching along the quay. He heard it come to a stop by the yacht and he heard one of the men give a shout which brought Kay out of the cabin. There followed a brief exchange of words and then the boat rocked a little as the man stepped down into the cockpit.

As far as Payne could tell only one of the men had come on board, so that it seemed the pattern of the operation was the same as before, the second man remaining by the jeep ready with the rifle if anyone tried to make a run for it. The sound of muffled voices came to Payne from the interior where the search was being made. It did not take long; in such a limited space it would not have been difficult to make sure that only two persons were on board. After a few minutes he heard a sound which he guessed was made by the man stepping out into the cockpit, no doubt still accompanied by Kay. The man said something which he failed to catch and he hoped that now he would go away.

But a moment later it became apparent that he was not yet satisfied. The fact that the boat was heeling over slightly to port and the sound of feet on the boards indicated that the man was moving towards the bows. Moreover, he must have had a torch and he was shining it here and there to assure himself that no one was hiding anywhere on deck. Not that there was really any place where a man could hide, but he was obviously a suspicious individual and was not going to take anything on trust.

Soon it was apparent to Payne that the man was standing in the bows almost immediately above him. He had come to a halt and was playing the torchlight on the surface of the water as if he half suspected that there might be someone down there. If he were to lean over the side and glance down he would be bound to catch sight of Payne's head; but for the moment he was not doing so.

It was touch and go for a time and Payne was afraid that the rope dangling from a cleat on deck might give the game away, but apparently the significance of this did not occur to the man; he switched the torch off, made his way back to the stern and left the boat. There was the sound of the jeep starting up and driving away, so it looked as though there were no more yachts to search and the operation was completed.

Kay came and helped him climb back on board. He stripped down in the saloon and dried himself on a towel provided by Diana. She watched him with interest but no embarrassment.

'You've got a good body,' she said.

Payne said nothing. He had taken off the money-belt and laid it on the table.

'So that's where you carry your valuables,' Kay said.

66

'What makes you think I have any valuables?'

'Well, you've got some money, I hope. Else how do we get paid?'

'Yes, I've got some money.'

'And something else, maybe?'

Kay was probing, but Payne had no intention of enlightening him. He would just have to contain his curiosity.

Kay said thoughtfully: 'With a gun and a knife you really mean to take care of what you've got, don't you?'

Payne gave him an accusing look. 'You've been poking through my pockets.'

Kay seemed unconcerned. 'Actually it was Di. She thought the jacket felt heavy. And you know what women are like: curious as cats.'

'And we all know what happened to the cat as a consequence.'

Diana smiled; she was as unconcerned as the man. 'We all have to die sometime.'

'Tell me,' Kay said, 'what have you really been doing in this country?'

Payne thought of telling him to mind his own business, but then he thought again and decided that there was no harm in revealing the truth.

'I was military instructor to the Palace Guard.'

Kay whistled softly. 'Cardona's crack troops. The last defenders of the old regime. That would make you a marked man, wouldn't it? How did you get away?'

'Never mind how.'

'Okay, skip it. But that's why they're looking for you, isn't it? That explains the searching of the boats.'

'Not necessarily. It could have been just routine.'

'But they haven't done it before. I'd say they could have been looking for somebody in particular.'

The same thought had occurred to Payne. But how had they learned of his escape? Through Colonel Diaz? Perhaps. But if Diaz wanted the diamond for himself, would he have given information about it to the revolutionaries? Probably not. They could, however, have discovered his escape when the palace was finally overrun. Either Espinosa or Salazar might have talked—if still alive.

'Well,' Kay said, 'it's obvious that you're a person of some importance, so we'd better take good care of you. And now I guess we could all do with some sleep. Tomorrow could be a long day.'

*   *   *

Payne slept little. He remained on the alert and he was awake when he heard the others stirring. It was still dark when they ate a hurried breakfast and it was only just growing light when they cast off from the quay and headed for the harbour mouth under the power of the auxiliary engine.

Kay was at the tiller and Diana was with him in the cockpit. Payne stayed below, keeping himself out of sight. He had sensed that the other two were a little on edge, though they were doing their best to appear unconcerned. It was understandable; if the boat were to be intercepted and it was discovered that they were smuggling a wanted man out of the country they could find themselves in big trouble.

But they cleared the estuary without incident and headed straight out to sea, still using engine power with the intention of putting the yacht beyond territorial waters with the least possible delay. It was a relief to Payne when Diana came into the saloon and told him that he could come out on deck.

'So we made it?'

'Looks like it. We're well away now and nobody can touch us. Take a look for yourself.'

He accepted the invitation and went up the steps to the cockpit where Kay was sitting with his hand on the tiller. The sun was shining brightly and the day was warming up. Payne gazed all round and could see no sign of land, just a wide expanse of water ruffled by a gentle breeze. To the south a ship was visible; it looked like a tanker, and there were some small craft with sails which could have been fishing-boats. It was all very peaceful, in sharp contrast to what life had been like recently ashore.

'What do you think of it?' Kay asked. 'Does it suit you?'

'Suits me fine. Now you just have to get me to Jamaica and we'll all be happy. How long do you think it'll take?'

'No telling. It'll be sailing from now on. Got to save the petrol for emergencies. If things go well we could be there in a few days. If they go badly, who knows?'

'Well, I'm not pressed for time. Just so long as we get there eventually.'

Kay grinned rather cynically. 'As far as it lies in the power of a mere mortal to guarantee a thing like that, I do. But as you very well know, they say prayers for those in peril on the sea, and there are hazards over which we have no control. If you feel like it you might send up a prayer or two for fair weather to the man in the sky.'

'I don't feel like it. I don't think it would make a hap'orth of difference, one way or the other.'

'And frankly,' Kay said, 'neither do I.'

Strangely, to Payne's way of thinking, the woman seemed to be disturbed by these exchanges.

'I don't think you should talk like that. It's asking for trouble.'

Kay spoke derisively. 'Gammon!' He turned to Payne. 'Would you believe it? She's superstitious.'

Payne looked at her. 'Is that so? Are you?'

'No,' she said. 'It's just that I don't think it's wise to tempt fate.'

'So what's that,' Kay demanded, 'if it's not superstition? It'll take more than a few words from us to alter the weather.'

'All right. Have it your own way.' She began to roll a cigarette.

She was an odd sort of person, Payne thought; a curious mixture: tough, hard-boiled perhaps; yet he got the impression that she was devoted to Kay, loved him maybe, though he was hardly a lovable character. And now it seemed she had this belief in a fate that could be tempted by a few light words uttered in jest. But were not some of the hardiest of seamen as superstitious as they came?

He decided it would be advisable not to do any whistling while they were at sea. She might throw him overboard as a Jonah.

* * *

A little later Kay stopped the engine and they hoisted sail. Payne helped. He knew the ropes; he had learnt to sail while stationed in Gibraltar during his army service. He offered to take his turn at the helm, which would make life easier for the other two. Kay accepted the offer after Payne had given a practical demonstration of his competence to handle a sailing-boat.

'I see that you're a man of many parts,' he said, with the merest hint of a sneer. 'You're not just a common or garden soldier-boy.'

'Maybe I'm not even that any more. It could be all behind me. Long ago and far away.'

'Othello's occupation's gone, eh? So what will you do now to earn an honest penny?'

'I'll manage somehow.'

'Maybe you have something in mind? Something to make you rich as Croesus perhaps?'

'No, nothing,' Payne said. He could tell that Kay was probing again; the man was obviously curious about him, possibly suspecting that there was rather more to this passenger than a mere soldier of fortune making a run for it when his side had lost the contest. 'I'll have to look for a job.'

Kay smiled disbelievingly. 'Not you. You're too much like me. You wouldn't be able to stand being tied down. Just imagine the nine to four routine day after day, sitting behind a desk waiting for the weekend when you can escape to the golf course and all that crap. It'd drive you crazy.'

'It wouldn't have to be a desk job.'

'True. But what qualifications have you got, except your knowledge of weaponry? Not much call for that in the business world.'

'I'll get by. Don't let it worry you.'

'Oh, I'm not worried. I'm just thinking

about you.'

'I'm touched by your concern for my welfare,' Payne said.

Kay laughed.

* * *

For two days the voyage progressed without incident of any importance. It would have been a wild exaggeration to describe *Vagabond* as a fast sailer, but she forged ahead in her own plodding manner and under the prompting of variable winds she made her way steadily if slowly eastward.

For the most part the weather was fine, the sun hot and few clouds in the sky. But occasionally a squall would suddenly come up out of nowhere, causing the boat to heel over and wetting the decks with large warm drops of rain. The duration of these squalls was seldom more than a few minutes; then the wind would die down, the rain would cease and the sun would burn away the moisture in no time at all.

Payne found himself enjoying the trip. After the almost constant danger to which he had been exposed of late it came as a great relief to be able to take things easy and just relax. The boat was a little haven of safety at the centre of this vast circle of pale blue water, with no sound but the creaking of the masts, the occasional crack of the sails, the breeze sighing in the rigging and the soft lapping of water against the moving hull. There were flying-fish shining like quicksilver in the sunlight, now and then a school of porpoises for company, and at night the coloured glow of phosphorescence where the water broke against the bows. Time meant nothing; it was as though he were living in a kind of vacuum in which nothing happened and nothing mattered. He would come out of it eventually, but for the present everything seemed to have slowed to the pace of this snail-like boat which went on its way, unhurried, unbothered, uncomplaining.

He found his companions pleasant enough to live with; they were both easygoing and appeared to take life as it came. They had had adventures, as anyone who travelled around the world in an ageing ketch was bound to have. Kay related the stories of some of these with wry humour; they had had brushes with authority here and there; perhaps this had been inevitable. He himself had on occasion been forced to cool his heels in a prison cell; but always he had managed to regain his liberty after a while, with the help mostly of some generous benefactor or other.

'I'm one of the children of Dame Providence. Things may look black at times, but always someone comes to the rescue.'

'As I did?'

He nodded. 'As you did.'

Payne wondered what they lived on. Surely

they could not depend wholly on the generosity of others. Perhaps they had some limited independent means. Perhaps they resorted to ways of replenishing the kitty that were not strictly legal. With a boat like this you could do a little in the smuggling line; drugs perhaps: heroin, cocaine, cannabis. He doubted whether they would be at all inhibited by qualms of conscience.

Anyway, he reflected, their honesty or possible lack of it was no concern of his.

It was on the evening of the third day that he was to discover just how wrong he was in this respect.

CHAPTER SIX

BARGAIN

He was taking his turn at the helm. The sky was full of stars and there was scarcely enough wind to fill the sails. He could have gone to sleep easily, but that would not have done at all; it would have been a dereliction of duty, and however balmy the air might be, however soporific the gentle motion of the boat, he had to stay awake.

Nevertheless, his eyelids were beginning to droop again and the sandman was working on him when Diana stepped out of the accommodation and joined him in the cockpit.

'Okay, Alan,' she said. 'I'll take over now.'

He became wide awake in an instant. But he was surprised.

'Why? It's not time yet.'

'I know. But George wants to have a word with you.'

It sounded odd to Payne. 'So why doesn't he come out here and talk? It's a fine night.'

'No,' she said. 'It has to be inside.'

There was something in her manner that set off a warning in his head. Strangely for her, she seemed not completely at ease, and he wondered why. He also wondered why Kay should have felt this sudden urge to have a talk with him. Had they not been talking to each other off and on ever since he had come aboard? So what was new?

'What's this all about?' he asked.

'He'll tell you.'

There could hardly be any question about that, and since she appeared unwilling to say anything more, he handed the tiller over to her and made his way down into the saloon.

The illumination in there was provided by a brass oil-lamp slung in gimbals. It gave a yellowish and not very brilliant light, but it was enough to reveal Kay sitting at the table with a collection of articles laid out in front of him. It was the sight of these objects that brought Payne to an abrupt halt.

'You bastard!' he said.

The articles on the table were the revolver, the flick-knife, his money-belt and the diamond. Even in the yellow light of the oil-lamp the gem sparkled with an astonishing brilliance.

'Well,' Kay said, not in the least put out, 'that's as may be. But sit down, won't you? We have matters to discuss.'

Payne sat down facing him. He saw that he had been too trusting; he had found the money-belt none too comfortable to wear all the time and had taken to leaving it with his other gear in the forward accommodation where he slept. He should have known better; he had had warning enough on the first day when Diana had searched the pockets of his jacket and found the weapons. Kay had not disguised his curiosity then regarding the contents of the money-belt, so it had been foolish to give him the opportunity to find out for himself the answer to his questions.

'I don't see what there is to discuss.'

'You don't? Oh, come now. What about that stone?' Kay stabbed a finger at the diamond. 'You aren't going to tell me it's just a piece of cut glass, are you?'

'I don't see why I should tell you anything about it. It's none of your damned business.'

'You think not? Well, that's a matter of opinion. And I happen to believe it's very much my business. You've been holding out on me, Alan. You didn't tell me you had anything like this in the belt.'

'Why should I?'

'Because it makes a difference, that's why. That's a diamond, isn't it?'

'You tell me.'

'Of course it is,' Kay said. 'And one that size must be worth a fortune. Not such a small fortune either. So now I ask myself what a guy like Alan Payne is doing with such a precious object. Are the services of a mercenary so highly valued these days that he gets paid off with a stone which wouldn't look out of place among the crown jewels?'

Payne said nothing. He thought of telling Kay the truth and then thought better of it. He might not have believed it, and why should he tell Kay anything? Let the bastard think what he liked.

'So you're not going to talk,' Kay said. 'All right, suit yourself. But my guess is you never got this for services rendered. In fact I don't believe it was ever given to you at all. I reckon you helped yourself. When you saw Cardona's lot were finished and you'd not only be out of a job but might even be stood up before a firing squad you decided to take whatever you could lay your hands on and skedaddle pretty damn quick.'

'And you think the diamond was just lying around waiting for me to pick it up?'

'Not just like that, no. Maybe you had to use some trickery to get it. I'm not asking how.'

'How very considerate of you.'

Kay grinned. 'Sarcasm will get you nowhere. Anyway, I can see now why you were being hunted back there. Whichever side was in power, they'd know all about this stone. It's probably famous. And I guess it wasn't a cast-iron secret that you'd made off with it. Maybe you had an accomplice who spilt the beans when they put the pressure on. Somebody who should've escaped with you but didn't make it. Got picked up and asked some questions. They know how to put the squeeze on in these parts, so I'm told. So that left you holding the baby—and what a baby! That the way it was?'

'You're doing the talking,' Payne said. 'But it's all guesswork, isn't it?'

'Sure it is. But it has to be something like that. Stands to reason. You have the sparkler; you were running away; you were being hunted. It all adds up.'

'So now what?'

'Now,' Kay said, 'I'm going to be generous. I'm going to make you an offer.'

'You want to buy the diamond off me? That's crazy. Where would you find the money?'

Kay shook his head. 'It would be crazy if that were the offer. But it's not. What I'm offering is a deal.'

Payne looked at him suspiciously. 'What kind of deal?'

'Fifty-fifty.'

'That's pretty cryptic. I don't get it. Enlighten me.'

'Half shares. You and me.'

Payne stared at him. 'You can't be serious.'

'For half a diamond the size of that one, who wouldn't be?'

'Well, it's not on. You must be able to see for yourself it's just not on. Whatever makes you think I'd agree to such a preposterous idea?'

'Doesn't seem to me to be all that preposterous. I'd say it's pretty generous on my part. I'll be splitting my half between Di and me, whereas if I'd been greedy I could have reckoned her as an equal partner and proposed a third each. That way you'd only have been getting a third. But like I said, I'm generous; I'm not planning to be too hard on you.'

'I'll say this for you, George,' Payne said, 'you've got a nerve. What makes you think you have a right to any share of the stone?'

Kay grinned again. 'Oh, that's an easy one. What's to prevent me handing you over to the police in Kingston and maybe getting a nice fat reward from the rich owners of the thing? I could, you know.'

'You could, but you won't. You wouldn't be sure of any reward and I don't think you're quite the type to do anything from a sense of civic duty.'

'*Touché*,' Kay said. 'So let's look at it from a different angle. I could kill you and take the lot.'

He had his right hand close to the revolver, but he was not actually touching it, and Payne did not feel any immediate threat to his life. Nevertheless, he realised it would be foolish to dismiss the possibility that Kay might do what he had suggested. The prize was such a valuable one that even murder might not appear too high a price to pay for it.

'You could,' he said. 'But I don't think you will.'

'You can't be sure though, can you?'

'No, I can't be sure.'

'I mean to say, disposal of the body would be no problem at all.' He made a gesture with his hand. 'Out there is the biggest grave of all; it's swallowed up its thousands, maybe its millions, and one more would make no difference whatever. There's no record of you ever coming aboard, so it'd be safe. Nothing could ever be pinned on Di or me, and we'd be rich. After all these years of living near the breadline it would make a pleasant change. You do see the attraction from our point of view, don't you?'

'Oh, yes, I see it clearly enough.'

'So why make things hard for yourself? Why force us to take an action we'd much rather not take? Why not agree to the terms?'

Payne thought of telling Kay he had got it wrong, that the diamond had not been stolen and that he was only a courier who had undertaken to deliver it to Cardona's daughter

81

in England. But even if Kay had believed the story, which was doubtful, it would have been unlikely to make any difference. He would not feel any obligation to see that the dead man's instructions were carried out. So, on reflection, maybe the best course would be to agree to his proposal. For the present.

'All right then. I can see you have me over a barrel.'

'So it's a deal?'

'It's a deal.'

'Sensible man. Now the question is, where do we sell the rock? I imagine you had something in mind?'

'Well,' Payne said, 'when it comes to a question of selling valuable jewels, there's just one place that springs immediately to mind. Amsterdam.'

'Ah!' Kay seemed to be giving it some thought. Then: 'It'd be a long voyage. We could make it, but it'd take time. No doubt you were planning something faster. An airline flight from Kingston, maybe?'

'Something like that.'

Kay did some more of the thinking, stroking his gingery beard and looking at Payne as if searching for any hint of double-dealing. Finally he said:

'We could still go along with that. Only change is, I'd be going with you and I'd be at your side when you did the selling. Not that I don't trust you, of course.'

'Oh, of course not.' Payne spoke with heavy irony. 'And Diana?'

'She could hang on in Kingston looking after the boat.'

'And you'd rejoin her there?'

'Naturally. You don't think I'd run out on her, do you?'

'The thought had crossed my mind.'

'Forget it. Me and Di, we're a team. We stick together through thick and thin.'

'I'm glad to hear it.'

Kay picked up the diamond and slipped it into his pocket. 'I'll hang on to this for the present. Just to be on the safe side.'

'I had a feeling you would,' Payne said. 'How about the gun?'

'That and the knife I think would be better out of the way. With weapons like those lying around in a confined space people are liable to get hurt.'

'So what are you going to do with them?'

'Throw them overboard. It's where all the garbage goes.' He picked up the revolver and the flick-knife. 'Like to see me do it? Just to make sure I'm not cheating.'

'Maybe I'd better.'

Kay went first and Payne followed. The light from the saloon gave some faint illumination to the cockpit where Diana was at the helm.

'Is it settled?' she asked.

'It's settled,' Kay said. 'Fifty-fifty. I'm just going to dispose of the hardware to avoid accidents. Watch this.'

He threw the revolver first. Payne heard the slight plop as it hit the water. Then the flick-knife went the same way. He felt no great sense of loss; he had always intended getting rid of them before going ashore in Kingston; he could not have taken them with him on the plane; they would have been detected and would have brought nothing but trouble. The diamond, of course, was a different matter. No one was going to suggest throwing that overboard.

'Farewell to arms,' Kay said. 'Now we're all pals together. And from here on in it's just plain sailing.'

To Diana this might have seemed like tempting fate again. But she did not say so, though she might have thought it. And if she had, she would maybe have been right. Except, of course, that it probably had nothing whatever to do with Kay's words, and fate would have taken a hand in the game whether tempted or not.

It was just one of those things.

CHAPTER SEVEN

TEMPTATION

It was just one of those things: a storm coming up out of the east, a storm that hit the ketch like a hammer in the night.

They had had no warning because the radio, like the rest of the equipment, was old and had broken down. So they had picked up no weather reports and could not in an emergency have sent out any calls for help. In some ways they were in the same situation as the early sailors in these waters: the Spanish galleons, the English privateers. They were out of touch with the shore and with any other vessels beyond the horizon.

There had been a flicker of lightning and a rumble of distant thunder, and this was all the indication they had had that all might not be well. But gradually the stars were blotted out, as though a vast black curtain were being drawn across the sky, and after a time they could hear the wind approaching like some wild beast released from its cage. The sea was feeling it and was moving uneasily, waves coming like fugitives fleeing from some unseen terror. The panic of the waves communicated itself to the yacht, which began to toss and roll uncontrollably.

'I don't like the look of this,' Kay said. 'We'd better get the canvas off her.'

Leaving Diana at the tiller, he and Payne set about furling the sails. As yet the wind had not really hit them with full power, but it was already lively, coming in gusts and throwing scuds of spray over the yacht. The lightning had become more brilliant and the thunder followed quickly with a sound like heavy guns firing.

On the heaving deck it was not easy to keep a footing, and in the darkness, relieved only by a little light coming from the saloon scuttles, one false step might have proved fatal, despite the standirons and wires that served as guard-rails around the yacht. The wind, increasing in strength from moment to moment, dragged at the sails, making them difficult to handle, and it was a struggle to secure them to the spars.

Then the rain came. It started almost hesitantly, a few large drops falling out of the now pitch-black sky and felt but not heard above the bluster of the wind. But these individuals, like the scouts of an advancing army, were soon to be followed by the main body. And this host of raindrops, when it came, fell with such intensity that it was if a vast cistern overhead had been tipped up to deposit its contents on this chosen area of sea. The wind drove it, so that it fell slantingly, beating against the two men who were struggling with the sails and threatening to hurl them into oblivion. They hung on with tooth and nail, drenched to the skin but ignoring all discomfort in what was indeed a fight for their very existence.

And finally the job was done, the canvas tamed, tightly bound and unable to break loose. Or so it was hoped.

They made their precarious way back to the cockpit where Diana was still clinging to the tiller, though there was little she could do to control the craft that was being driven by the storm. The seas were rising and the yacht had become the plaything of the waves; one moment it was tossed high on a crest, the next it was sliding down into the trough that followed. Water was slopping over into the cockpit and to Payne it seemed a perilous situation; if they did not keep the boat's head to the sea a bigger wave breaking over the stern could finish them.

Kay apparently had the same thought in his mind, for he shouted: 'We'll have to put out a sea-anchor.'

Payne knew what that was: a kind of canvas bag shaped like a cone with an iron ring to keep it open. This would be trailed from the bows to act as a brake and ensure that the craft remained heading into the wind. Sometimes it was used to check a boat's drifting, and in the absence of anything better a bucket on a rope could be used to serve the purpose.

In this case, however, there was no need for the bucket. Kay opened a locker and fetched out the drogue. He shouted to Payne to accompany him and, leaving Diana still with the tiller in her grasp, they again made their way forward, advancing from one desperate handhold to the next. It was no great distance, only a few yards in fact, but each foot had to be fought for as the rain-laden wind tore at them with invisible fingers that strove to pluck them from their footing on the deck and fling them willy-nilly into the raging sea.

But they made it. They reached the bows where rails, converging to a point, gave them some feeling of security. Here Kay made the end of the rope fast to bitts fixed to the deck while Payne held the drogue. With the rope secured, the two of them eased the drogue under the rails and lowered it into the water. It filled immediately and in a moment had drawn out the full length of line and stretched it tight. The effect was all that could have been desired: the yacht came round head to wind and stayed so. The danger of being pooped by a following sea was past.

Yet in this very moment of success the disaster was to occur. Kay, perhaps momentarily relaxing his vigilance, was leaning over the rails as if trying to peer into the darkness into which the drogue had gone when a heavier than usual roll of the yacht caused him to lose both his balance and his grip. It all happened in an instant, so that there was nothing Payne could do to save him. Indeed, he was scarcely aware of what was happening; he knew only that one moment Kay was there and the next he had gone, uttering one last despairing cry as he plunged to his death.

Payne clung to the rails and tried to pierce the enveloping darkness with his gaze. A flicker of lightning threw everything into stark relief for a moment, the plunging boat with its bare masts, the foam-capped waves, the marbled hollows, the inky clouds above, the teeming rain and the ghostly drifting spindrift. He thought he caught a glimpse of a hand and an arm lifted as if in a last gesture of farewell, or perhaps in a vain appeal for help. Then the light vanished and he saw no more.

It was the last of Kay. He stood there, hands still gripping the upper rail, letting the fact sink into his brain, the fact that Kay was lost, swallowed by what he himself had described as the biggest grave of them all. Maybe the sharks would make a meal of him; maybe he would sink to those cold depths where the sun never shone and strange sea creatures lived amongst the ooze and the slime and the hulks of long lost ships. Well, he was gone now, gone for good and all. So goodbye George, goodbye for ever.

And then suddenly another thought came into Payne's head, and stunned him. It was the realisation that in going Kay had taken something with him and that that too was lost.

The diamond!

Kay had put it in his pocket for safe-keeping, and that was the irony of it. Still, in a way, you might say he had succeeded only too well, because it was a dead certainty that no other people would ever get their hands on it now. It was his for ever, wherever he might be. And much good might it do him.

Payne turned and clawed his way back to the stern. Diana was still there, just as he had left her; she had not moved. She looked up at him as he stepped down into the cockpit, and then her gaze moved past him as if searching for someone else.

He realised with something of a shock that she was ignorant of what had happened. She had seen nothing and heard nothing. That last cry that Kay had uttered would have been drowned by the racket of the storm and she did not know that he was gone. Now he, Payne, would have to break the news to her, would have to reveal to her the bitter fact of her man's death. It was a dreadful thing to have to do, and he stood there, hanging on, tongue-tied, while the lightning flickered and the thunder cracked, while the wind tore at them with its banshee wailing and the rain bucketed down.

It was she who spoke first. 'Where is George?'

He made a hopeless kind of gesture with his hand, and it was enough. She guessed.

She gave a cry. He had never heard a sound like it before. It might have been a soul in agony given voice. It cut through the clamour of the storm and penetrated to his heart.

'I'm sorry.'

Sorry! What a feeble word! And what was his sorrow to her?

'No,' she cried. 'Oh, no, no, no! It can't be. It can't.'

She stood up, as if she would have gone to search for him, but Payne laid a hand on her arm and restrained her.

'It's no use. He's gone.'

She sank back on to the seat. The tiller swung and caught her in the side, but she seemed not to feel it. She looked up at him and there was accusation in her voice.

'You!'

He knew what she meant. And perhaps she had reason to suspect him. For, after all, he had some cause for resentment against Kay and might have seized the chance to take revenge. And this was what had evidently come into her mind. He hastened to exonerate himself.

'No. You're wrong. I had nothing to do with it. It was an accident. He fell. I didn't touch him.'

She was silent. He was not sure she believed him. He said: 'You can't suppose I pushed him overboard. Even if I had wanted to kill him, which I did not, would I have done that, knowing that he had the diamond in his pocket? It would have been a crazy thing to do.'

The logic of this must have got through to her. When she spoke again it was in a more reasonable tone of voice. The grief was still there, the anguish even, but she had herself under control.

'Yes, you are right. But how could he? I mean he was not a fool. He'd had so much experience.'

'Anyone can make a slip. It takes only a moment. An instant's lack of care, of attention, and it's all over. There's no second chance. I truly am sorry.'

* * *

With the sea-anchor doing its job the yacht was in less danger of being swamped, but a lot of water had been shipped and Payne got to work with the bilge-pump. The worst was now past and the wind was gradually abating. The tiller had been lashed in a central position and it looked as if the yacht would ride out the storm without further trouble.

But the tragedy lay like a cloud on the two survivors. It was Diana who felt it most, as was only natural. But Payne could not fail to be affected also; and not simply because of the loss of the diamond. For in spite of Kay's double-dealing he had had a certain liking for the man. He had undoubtedly been a bit of a rogue, but there had been something about him that had touched a chord in Payne and induced a fellow-feeling; one adventurer for another.

He spoke to Diana about Kay, sensing that it might be good for her to talk rather than to keep everything bottled up, brooding over her loss.

'You had been together for a long time, I suppose?'

'Yes, a very long time.'

'He told me you were a team. Like to tell me about it?'

'No.'

'Fair enough.'

But two minutes later she began to talk, and then it all came out in a flood: the things they had done together, the places they'd been to, the adventures they'd had. She smoked those filthy hand-rolled cigarettes as she talked, one after another, and he let her go on, let her pour it all out until she stopped, perhaps from sheer exhaustion.

'I must be boring you,' she said.

'No. I'm fascinated. You've had a very full life.'

'With him, yes. But now—' Her shoulders seemed to droop in an expression of hopelessness.

'What will you do?'

'I don't know. I haven't even begun to think about it yet.'

He had a feeling that she would manage.

Kay's death was a terrible blow to her, that was not to be doubted; but he did not believe she would allow herself to be completely crushed by it, as some women might. She was tough and would make a new life for herself; he was sure of it.

* * *

By morning the storm had passed. The sun shone on them from an almost cloudless sky and the sea, though not in a flat calm, had lost the ferocity of the previous night. There was a light breeze, and they hoisted the sails and proceeded on the voyage, leaving George Kay in the grave which had no headstone to mark the spot.

Two days later they slipped unobtrusively into Kingston harbour with sails furled and engine running, on one side the old fort on the hill and on the other Port Royal, where Henry Morgan used to roister with his buccaneering crew before earthquake came to devastate the place.

There were formalities, of course: the usual checks for health and contraband, complicated in this instance by the loss of the yacht's owner. There were questions to be answered, statements to be made, documents signed. The fact that they had come from a country recently taken over by revolutionary forces appeared to give rise to some suspicion, especially with the further complication of Payne's presence on board, which seemed to be entirely unofficial and unrecorded.

But all was smoothed out eventually. The yacht was made fast to a jetty and the two occupants were given permission to go ashore.

Payne did not leave Kingston at once. There seemed to be no point in hurrying his departure; perhaps no point in his journey at all, now that the diamond was lost. So for the present he made the yacht his hotel while he explored the town and made sorties into the hinterland of the Blue Mountains and other parts, sometimes on his own, but more often in the company of Diana.

He was pleased to observe that she was recovering her spirits, shaking off the depression that had come upon her after George Kay's death.

'He would not have wanted me to mope,' she said, as if excusing herself for coming so quickly as it were out of mourning. 'Life has to go on.'

Once again he asked the question: 'What will you do now? I suppose the boat comes to you?'

'Yes. He made a will leaving all he had to me. He insisted on it. Not that there's anything much besides the boat.'

'Will you continue to sail in her?'

'I think not. It wouldn't be the same.'

They were sitting in the saloon, drinking rum and coke, Diana smoking another of her foul cigarettes. In the harbour were ships loading cargoes of bananas, pineapples, sugar, coffee; a pleasure liner anchored in the bay, tourists being ferried ashore in boats...

'No,' Payne said, 'I suppose not.' And then: 'I owe you some money.'

She looked surprised. 'What money?'

'Seven hundred and fifty dollars. The second half of the agreed fare for my passage.'

'So you're going to pay me?'

'Naturally. It was a bargain.'

'The bargain was with George.'

'You are his successor.'

'Yes, but he took the diamond from you. I'd say that relieves you of any obligation to keep your side of the contract.'

'I'm dealing with you now,' Payne said, 'not him.' He took a wad of dollars from his pocket and laid it on the table. 'I think you'll find it's all there. You can count it if you like.'

'I don't want to.' She left the money where it was, not touching it, as if some inhibition prevented her from doing so.

'The diamond wasn't mine, you know,' Payne said.

'Ah! So you did steal it?'

'No; that isn't what I meant. It was Cardona's. He entrusted it to me to take to his daughter in England. It was to be his last gift to her. Now, of course, she'll never get it, because the courier lost it.'

The woman was staring at him. 'So that's the

way it was. I didn't realise.'

'No, of course you didn't. You thought I was a thief.'

She looked embarrassed. 'Well—'

'I'm not, you know. I have my faults but dishonesty is not one of them.'

'So now what will you do? Will you go to her without the diamond and tell her how it was lost?'

'I've been wondering about that, and I think I must, if only to assure her that her father was thinking of her just before he died. I shall have to explain to her that I made a hash of things.'

She took a drag on the cigarette, sucked in the smoke and let it drift from her mouth, not giving a damn about her lungs. She said softly: 'Perhaps you won't have to do that.'

He failed to see what she was driving at. 'What do you mean?'

'This,' she said. She reached into a pocket and pulled out an object which she placed on the table beside the pile of dollars.

Payne stared at it in disbelief.

'It's real,' she said. 'Take it.'

He did so. It was the diamond sure enough.

'You had it all the time?'

'Yes. George gave it to me to keep. He said it was in case anything happened to him. It was as if he had a premonition of what was to come. Though I suppose you'll say that's just nonsense. All the same, seeing the way it's worked out—'

'But I still don't see why you waited until now to tell me. Why not at once? You led me to believe it was lost with him. Why?'

'Perhaps out of spite. I was hating you then just for being still alive when George was dead. Perhaps it was a way of punishing you.'

'I see. But you don't hate me now?'

'No.'

'I'm glad,' he said. And then: 'Were you going to keep it?'

'I thought about it,' she admitted. 'I couldn't make up my mind. It was a great temptation.'

'You would never have done it.'

'Perhaps not.' She had the flat tin out again and was rolling another cigarette, which she lit from the butt of the previous one. There were nicotine stains on her fingers and she had a dry smoker's cough and a husky voice. 'But I did really think about it. I'd have been rich.'

'I don't think it would have done you any good. I've an idea this diamond is bad news for whoever has it. Lots of people have probably died because of it. Cardona had it, and see what happened to him.'

'Without the diamond it would have happened just the same.'

'Maybe.'

'You're surely not telling me you think there's a curse on it or something like that? You don't believe in that sort of thing, do you?'

'Not really, no. But the sheer value of the stone could have the effect of a curse. People will do almost anything to get their hands on it.'

'And yet you're going to take it to this girl—what's her name?'

'Maria.'

'You're not worried that it might mean trouble for her?'

He thought about it, asking himself whether it might not have been better if the diamond had indeed gone overboard with Kay. What use was a stone like that really? Its value lay only in its rarity. And did this girl, Maria, need it? Cardona had said that he had not heard from her in two years, yet she had presumably been managing somehow. So she would not feel the loss of the gem if it never came to her, because she would be unaware that it should have been hers. What you've never had you never miss.

He looked thoughtfully at the woman. Suppose he were to go through with the fifty-fifty deal he had agreed to with Kay. The man was no longer there to benefit from it, but his partner was. Why not forget about Maria and share the proceeds of the sale with Diana? It would make both of them rich.

But then it occurred to him that if he was going to cheat Maria anyway and welsh on his promise to Cardona, why not go the whole hog and take the lot for himself? Then he could send for Isabel Romero and they could both live very happily together on the price of the stone.

Except that he would not be happy. He would be plagued with an uneasy conscience. Cardona had chosen him as the courier because he felt sure he could trust him, and for that reason alone it was impossible for him to play the cheat. The temptation was very great, as it had been for Diana, but like her he felt obliged in the end to reject it. Maria had to have the diamond.

The woman seemed to have been reading his thoughts, smoking her cigarette and watching him, saying nothing.

Now she said: 'You've decided, haven't you? You've thought about all the money you could get in Amsterdam and you've reached a decision.'

'Yes.'

'So what's it to be?'

'I have to deliver the stone.'

She nodded. 'It's what I thought. When will you go?'

'Tomorrow.'

'I shall miss you,' she said.

CHAPTER EIGHT

HELP

It was raining when he left the plane at Heathrow. He had discarded the money-belt in Kingston and was carrying his cash in a wallet. The diamond was in a pocket. If he had been body-searched it would have been discovered, but he had taken the risk and had gone through the customs without trouble.

Summer was coming to an end and he felt the autumnal chill in the air. It was his first experience of grey English skies for years, but in spite of the weather he was glad to be back. He had moved around, seen many places, but this after all was home and there was nowhere else in the world quite like it.

The first thing he did was establish a base to work from. It was a room in a modest Bayswater hotel. He took up residence there and on the second day went on an expedition to find the address that Cardona had given him.

It turned out to be a maisonette in Fulham. It was a very narrow property, having been formed by dividing the original house down the middle and adding an extra front door. The door was painted blue and there was a bell-push on the right which Payne stabbed a few times with his thumb. He got no result from the exercise and had to come to the conclusion that there was no one at home. He decided to try again later and had just turned away when a young woman met him head-on and they both came to a halt.

'Oh,' she said, 'were you looking for someone?'

She was wearing a long white raincoat and a beret with blonde hair showing below it, and she was carrying a leather shoulder-bag and a couple of polythene bags with groceries in them. Her face was rather bony and she had a wide mouth and a pair of buckteeth, but she was far from repulsive. Payne thought she had nice friendly eyes and he put her age at not much over twenty.

'Do you live here?' he asked.

'Yes, I do.'

'You're not Miss Cardona, are you?' There was nothing about her that looked the least bit Latin-American. She was typically English.

'No,' she said. 'I'm Joanna Parrish. So it's Maria you're looking for?'

'Yes. My name is Alan Payne. I was given this address.'

'Who by?'

'Her father.'

'Oh, I see.' She gave him a careful inspection, as though weighing him up and trying to decide whether he could be trusted; and apparently he passed the test because she said: 'I think you'd better come inside. We can't talk out here.'

He moved aside so that she could get past him to the door and waited.

'Hold these,' she said, handing him the bags of groceries. 'I've got to unlock.'

He took the polythene bags and she hunted in the shoulder-bag and came up with the key. He was still holding the bags when she ushered him in and closed the door. They were in a tiny entrance hall where there was hardly room for the two of them to turn round, but she got herself out of the coat and the beret and hung them on one of the wooden pegs fixed to a wall. Then she led him into a living-room which gave every evidence of female occupation: comfortable but a trifle art-crafty and faintly scented.

'I'll take those now,' she said. She had deposited her shoulder-bag on a side-table and she relieved Payne of the groceries and took them into a kitchen which he caught a glimpse of through an open door. It looked very well equipped in a limited space.

When she came back she invited him to sit down and indicated an armchair. She herself relaxed on a sofa, the kind that could be converted into a bed if the need arose. She had on a plain grey dress of some close-fitting ribbed material, with long sleeves and a crew neck. The dress was short, which was no problem for her because she had marvellous legs, one of which she tucked underneath her as she sat on the sofa.

'She doesn't live here any more, I'm afraid.'

'Oh,' Payne said. It was not altogether unexpected. It would have been too much to hope that his errand would be completed so easily. 'But she did?'

'Oh, yes. We used to share the place.'

'But not now?'

'No. She decided to make a move.'

'Any particular reason?'

'The usual one. A man.'

'I see. And I suppose she's living with him now?'

'I don't really know. We haven't been in touch lately. Fact is, we had a bit of a row and we haven't communicated since.'

'What was the row about?'

'Garry.'

'Garry being the man?'

'Yes. I told her she was an idiot to get mixed up with a guy like him, because anybody with half an eye could see he was a no-good bastard and mean with it.'

'And I suppose she didn't like you saying that?'

'What do you think? For some reason or other she'd fallen for him, hook, line and sinker. It was so strange, because until then I'd always thought of her as being pretty level-headed. And then to go off the rails for a heel like him. Didn't make sense.'

'Do things like that ever make sense? It's an illogical emotion, isn't it? Love.'

She gave him a faintly amused look. 'Speaking from experience?'

Payne grinned. 'It's what I've been told.'

'Anyway, it became something of a slanging match, and then she moved out and I haven't seen her since.'

'When was this?'

'Oh, about three months ago.'

'And you're living on your own now?'

'For the present, yes.'

Payne saw that he had come up against a snag. He had brought the diamond to London, not without a fair amount of difficulty, but now he had no idea where the girl he was to deliver it to was hanging out. She might be anywhere.

'You're not the first one, you know,' Miss Parrish said.

'Not the first?'

'There was another man who came here asking for Maria two days ago. He said his name was Gonzalez. I didn't much like the look of him, so I didn't invite him in.'

'What did he look like?'

She gave a brief description. 'Lean, average height, hollow cheeks, dark complexion, black moustache. Spoke with a foreign accent. Know anyone who fits that picture?'

'Yes, I do. But his name isn't Gonzalez; it's Diaz. Colonel Bernardo Diaz.'

It had to be him. Having failed to prevent the courier getting away with the diamond, he must have decided to take a flight to England and pick up the trail there. He would have known the London address where Maria had been staying and had made a check on it.

'Who is this Colonel Diaz?' Miss Parrish asked.

'He was on the military staff of President Cardona, Maria's father, before the revolutionaries took over. Perhaps you heard about that?'

'Well, yes. There was something about it on TV and in the papers. Normally I don't take much interest in what goes on in that part of the world; I'm not a political animal. But it caught my attention because of Maria. I wondered how it would affect her. But I still don't see why this man, Diaz, would be looking for her.'

'Actually, I'd say it's me he's looking for. He'd be hoping she could give him a lead.'

'You'll have to explain that. Why is he looking for you and how could she help?'

Payne wondered whether to tell her the whole story. What harm could it do? And besides, it occurred to him that he might use her help in tracing Maria, and he was more likely to gain her co-operation if he took her into his confidence. In the end he decided to tell her a part of it.

'I'm a courier. I've been entrusted with something rather valuable, a last gift from Cardona to his daughter. Incidentally, he's dead now. But I expect you heard that too.'

'Yes.'

'Well, Diaz wasn't in favour of sending the gift and he was even less in favour of me being the one chosen to deliver it. I think he tried to get at me before I left the country, and now he's planning to nail me here before I can hand over the goods. Or if he's too late for that he'll almost certainly have a go at Maria.'

'To get the gift for himself?'

'That's about it. He's a greedy man and a dangerous one. He wouldn't stop at murder even. Human life doesn't count for much with him. Especially if the life happens to be standing in the way of his interests.'

She looked concerned. He doubted whether the concern was for him, so it had to be for Maria, even though they had parted on less than amicable terms.

'How,' she asked, 'did you come to be involved? What were you doing down there?'

'I was working for President Cardona.'

'In what capacity?'

'As a soldier.'

'Ah!' she said; and he sensed a hint of disapproval. 'A mercenary.'

'I suppose you might call it that.'

'What would you call it?'

'Military adviser perhaps.'

'It adds up to the same thing in the end, doesn't it? You were helping a tyrant maintain his grip on power. Is that a very honourable way of making a living?'

'I can think of worse,' Payne said. 'And for someone who professes not to be a political animal I get the impression that you have some pretty strong views on certain aspects of the subject.'

'I just don't think people should make money by killing other people. It's—well—immoral.'

'Well, that's a good basic principle, I suppose. And I won't get into an argument about it. Does it mean I'm no longer welcome here? Are you asking me to leave?'

'No,' she said. 'Don't be in such a hurry. You interest me. I'd like to find out what makes a mercenary tick. And besides, I'm bothered about Maria. She ought to be warned about this Colonel Diaz, don't you think?'

'Yes, I do. But how do I find her? That's the question.'

'Um! We'll have to give some thought to it.' She stood up suddenly. 'Would you like a cup of coffee?'

He was glad to see that he appeared to be no longer beyond the pale, and he accepted without hesitation. She went off to make the coffee and was back within minutes with two mugs on a tray.

'This man calling himself Gonzalez,' Payne said. 'Did you tell him about Garry?'

'No. I just told him Maria had gone away and I didn't know where. Then he asked me if anyone else had been inquiring about her recently, and I told him nobody had. I expect it was you, he meant.'

'You can be sure of that. And then he went away?'

'Yes.'

'He didn't say why he was looking for Maria?'

'No. And I didn't ask. I just wanted to be rid of him.'

Payne drank some coffee, thinking. He had a problem. How did you set about finding someone in a city as big as London? Call in the police to help? He had no wish to do that; he felt it would be better not to get involved with the officers of the law. So where did he start? He looked at the girl, again sitting on the sofa, a cup of coffee in her hand, and it seemed to him that she was still his best hope.

'I suppose,' he said, 'it would be too much to ask you to help me find Maria?'

'So you want me to give up some of my valuable time to get you out of your difficulty. Is that it?'

'You can always say no.'

'Of course I can.' And then she gave a laugh and said: 'But the fact is my time isn't terribly valuable just at present, because I'm out of a job. I've been working for a travel agency, but they've gone out of business and I'm one of the army of unemployed. I'm looking round for something else, but things are difficult, especially with no one to share the expenses of this place.'

'I suppose so.' The house was far from large but he guessed the rent was high, situated where it was.

'Mind you,' she said, 'I'm not on my beam-ends. I've got some capital and if things get really tough I can always take the begging-bowl to my loving father, who's got plenty. But I don't want to do that if I can avoid it. I like to be independent.'

'I can understand that,' Payne said. He supposed she would be drawing money from the DSS too, but that would probably not be enough to finance her life style. 'And there's no one else?'

She took his meaning very quickly. 'You're thinking about a boyfriend? Well, there's no one at present; no one really close. There was Paul, but we split up, decided we just weren't made for each other after all. It happens.'

'Yes, it happens.'

There was a musing look in her eye, as though she were thinking about the way it had happened. Then suddenly she appeared to come back to the present with a start.

'But my God!' she said. 'Why am I telling you all this? I hardly know you, and here I am baring my soul.' She gave an embarrassed laugh. 'You must be the sort women confide in. Are you?'

'I've never imagined so. But I'm a good

listener.'

'Well, let's get back to business. I think maybe the best plan would be to look for Garry. Find him and we'll find Maria. That's if she hasn't found out what a louse he is and thrown him over.'

Payne gathered from this that she had agreed to help him.

And then he had a thought. 'Couldn't we just look him up in the phone book? He's probably in there.'

'He may be. But there's just one snag. I don't know his surname. He's always been referred to just as Garry. No good looking that up, is there?'

He had to admit the truth of that.

CHAPTER NINE

TAIL

It was past noon, and Payne suggested that it might not be a bad idea if he were to take Joanna out to lunch.

'Afterwards we can start hunting. What do you say?'

She had no objection and they left the house together. He was keeping his eyes skinned for any sign of Diaz. It was possible that the man might be watching the place to see if he turned up. But it would hardly have been possible for anyone on his own to maintain a permanent watch, and in fact there appeared to be no one looking at all like Diaz lurking in the vicinity.

Joanna must have observed his wariness, for she said: 'Are you looking for that man?'

He admitted that he was. 'I'd rather see him before he sees me.'

'But you haven't seen him?'

'No.'

'Perhaps he's given up.'

Payne thought it unlikely. The diamond would have too strong a hold on him. Eventually he might give up, but not yet, not for a long time yet. Meanwhile, it would be wise not to relax one's vigilance.

The street in which the maisonette was situated was a quiet one; it was in fact a narrow connecting link between two avenues, not far from the river. Not much commercial traffic used it, and the residence of the Bishop of London was little more than a quarter of a mile away.

Payne and Joanna had lunch in a restaurant in Chelsea, just off the King's Road. It was a place she knew and recommended, and he left the decision to her, since his own knowledge of London was limited. He enjoyed the meal; he enjoyed being with her. He thought she would be fun to go around with. But she was years younger than he was and he wondered just how he appeared in her eyes, even if you ignored that mercenary tag she had pinned on him.

She had class; it was apparent in the way she spoke, in her manner. But he was on an equal footing in that respect because he had probably come from a similar kind of background. His father was a partner in an old-established law firm in a country town in Berkshire and was in comfortable financial circumstances. He had made sure that his son had the right kind of education and had expected him to make a career in the legal profession. But this particular son had been a disappointment; he had an adventurous streak in him and had run off and enlisted in the army.

Fortunately for the father's peace of mind, there was a younger son who was more amenable to parental guidance and would one day become a barrister. Payne realised that he himself was regarded as the black sheep of the family, but he did not let it worry him. He had had very little correspondence with any of his relations for years.

During lunch he questioned Joanna about Maria. 'What was she doing in England?'

She seemed surprised that he did not know. 'Weren't you told?'

'I was told practically nothing. Cardona said he hadn't been in touch with her for some time, but that was all.'

'She was studying at the London School of Economics until she dropped out.'

'Why did she do that?'

'It was all to do with this conscience thing.'
Payne was fogged. 'Conscience! How did that come about?'

'Oh, she got mixed up with this lefty crowd and they opened her eyes to the evil things her father was doing back there in her home country. They convinced her that it was the revolutionaries, the freedom fighters, who were the good guys and that Cardona's lot were the villains. And of course the real arch villain, the devil incarnate, was dear old daddy. After that she decided she couldn't possibly accept anything more from him, and that included a place at the LSE. So she just dropped out.'

'That must have been when she broke off communication with Cardona, I suppose.'

'Yes. He'd been giving her a nice fat allowance which was paid into a London bank account, but she gave up drawing on that too. In her book it had become dirty money squeezed out of the blood of the oppressed peasantry.'

'Well, there won't be any more going into that account now.'

'I suppose not.'

'So what was she living on?'

'This and that. Odd jobs. Anything she could find. She couldn't draw social security benefit because she isn't British, you see. She was outside the system. Never had been in it.'

Payne guessed that Joanna had given her

some help, maybe waiving the other girl's contribution to the living expenses, until the intervention of a man had led to the breaking up of the female partnership.

'Was Garry in the group that converted her?'

'Oh, good lord, no. His relations with that lot were strictly commercial.'

'So what does he do for a living?'

'That's a good question. He doesn't appear to have any regular job, but he never seems to be short of money. He's the sort of man who can get practically anything for you, cheap. He tried to sell me a wrist-watch once; genuine Rolex, brand-new at a giveaway price.'

'But you didn't buy it?'

'No. When I buy something I like to know that the vendor has come by it honestly.'

'Are you telling me Garry is bent?'

'As a corkscrew.'

'You mentioned this to Maria perhaps?'

'Oh, yes. It was all part of the row we had. She refused to believe it, accused me of slandering him just because I didn't like him. How can anyone be so blind? He's a real charmer, of course, no doubt about that. And smooth as they come. Maybe she'll get wise to him one day. The affair is bound to end in tears one way or another. The mystery is why he bothered with her, though she's attractive enough, I must admit. But there must have been more in it than that. My guess is he was counting on making a profit on the deal.'

'You mean because she was President Cardona's daughter?'

'Yes. He'd have figured out that there'd be plenty to come from that source.'

'But if she'd renounced all that—'

'Maybe he didn't know. Or maybe he thought he could make her change her mind and start drawing on the funds again. And maybe he's done just that; in a tussle between her conscience and Garry he could have been the one that came out on top.'

'Well, he'll know now there's no chance of any more coming to her from Cardona.'

'Unless he had money salted away in overseas bank deposits which Maria would inherit.'

'I suppose that is a possibility. Though I don't know quite what the legal position would be. I imagine the new government might lay claim to all his assets.'

'But now there's this gift you've brought for her. It's valuable, you say?'

'Very valuable.'

She looked thoughtful. 'That could raise complications, couldn't it? First, will she accept the gift, coming from him? Second, if she does, will Garry get his dirty paws on it?'

Payne had to agree that these were questions yet to be answered. 'But from my point of view it makes no difference. I've still got to find her and hand it over to her. If she decides to throw it away, that's up to her. My job will be done.'

'And that's all that concerns you?'

'What else should?'

'Nothing, I suppose. You'll have done your duty. But tell me, Alan, did you have much difficulty in getting here with the gift?'

'Frankly,' he said, 'I had one hell of a job.'

'And it was at the risk of your life?'

'Yes. I came close to being shot and close to being drowned.'

'And after all that are you going to tell me you'd be perfectly happy to see whatever it is you were risking everything to deliver passing straight into the hands of a swine like Garry? Honestly, now.'

She was right, of course. It would be just too damned galling for words if he had gone through so much simply for the benefit of a smart operator who had done nothing to earn the prize. And what a prize it was! But what could he do? Keep the thing for himself? He had thought of that before and had rejected it. Now he rejected it again.

'I have to do what I undertook to do.'

'Ah!' she said. 'You are a man of your word, I see.'

He was not sure whether she had spoken in praise or in mockery. He rather suspected the latter.

*   *   *

They had no luck in the search that day. They

trawled certain coffee-bars and pubs and other places where Gary might have put in an appearance, but there was no sign of him. It was pretty late when Payne left Joanna at her maisonette. She did not invite him in, and they parted on the doorstep, having arranged to meet again on the following day and continue the search.

He walked to Putney Bridge tube station, staying on the alert for any glimpse of Diaz but seeing nothing of him. There were not many people about and the only person he took any note of was a man in a blue trenchcoat and one of those country style hats in a check tweed material. He noticed this man because he was standing in a position from which he could get a good view of Joanna's front door on the opposite side of the street. And why would anybody be standing there at that time of night? Perhaps he had an appointment to meet somebody in that particular place, but this seemed unlikely. The hat was pulled down and the light was none too good, making it impossible to get a good view of his face, but he was not very tall and appeared to be of slight build.

He was still there when Payne, having said good-night to Miss Parrish, walked back down the street. He was smoking a cigarette and Payne caught the odour of the smoke as he passed, after crossing the street in order to bring himself on to the same side as the man. In passing he turned his head and stared hard at this lounger and could just make out the shadowy lineaments of the face under the tweed hat. The man did not meet his gaze; he was staring at the ground as if to avoid any eye contact, and he was certainly not Diaz; he was a complete stranger.

Payne continued on his way. He turned a corner to the right, proceeded for about two hundred yards and came out on to the Fulham Palace Road. Glancing back he caught sight of the man in the blue trenchcoat and the tweed hat no more than forty yards behind. Payne quickened his pace, but when he came to the Fulham Road junction another backward glance assured him that the man was still not far behind. He crossed over into Fulham High Street where there were more people about, but the man was keeping in touch and there could be no doubt at all that he was doing a tailing job. Curiously enough, he appeared to be making no effort to disguise the fact, so either he was a novice at the game or he just did not give a damn whether the person being tailed was aware of the fact or not.

When Payne got into the tube train at Putney Bridge he was not at all surprised to see the man in the blue trenchcoat getting in after him; he had been expecting nothing less. There were not many passengers in the coach and the man took a seat where he was in full sight of Payne, though he seemed studiously to avoid looking directly at him.

Payne on the other hand stared hard at the man and was able to get a clearer view of his face. It was not very impressive; there was a starved look about it and the nose was sharply pointed, the mouth small and overshadowed by a wispy moustache.

When the train came to Bayswater, Payne got out. The man in the trenchcoat followed him. Outside the station Payne set out to walk the quarter mile or so to the hotel where he was staying. The man fell in behind him as before.

Payne came to a corner and turned left into a quiet side-street. Having taken half a dozen paces he stopped abruptly, got his back to a wall where the light was poor and waited. He did not have to wait long; he heard the patter of feet, indicating that his follower was hurrying, and the man appeared suddenly round the corner. He seemed unaware that Payne was there until he drew level, and it must have come as a shock to him when his right arm was seized and twisted up behind his back.

'Now,' Payne said, 'tell me what you're up to.'

The man said nothing. After one startled cry he had fallen silent. He was making a vigorous effort to free himself, but Payne increased the pressure on his arm and he gave another cry, this time of agony, and gave up struggling.

'That's better,' Payne said. 'Now let's have it. Why have you been tailing me?'

'Tailing you!' The man tried to sound surprised, but it was a poor try. 'I dunno wotcher mean.'

'Sure you do. You've been on my tail all the way from Fulham. So what's the game?'

'You're wrong. I'm on me way home.'

'Do you want me to break your arm?' Payne asked. 'I could do it, you know.'

'Okay,' the man said in a sulky tone of voice. 'I have been following you.'

'Why?'

'Because that's what I'm being paid to do, innit?'

'What do you mean, being paid to do? Who's paying you?'

'The client, of course. I'm a private investigator.' Payne began to understand. 'A private eye, eh? So what's your name, gumshoe?'

'Raggler.'

'And who's the client?'

'I can't tell you that. It's confidential.'

'You really do want your arm broken, don't you?' Payne applied some extra pressure again, bringing another squeal from the private eye. 'Was it a man called Diaz?'

'Nah. I never heard of anybody of that name.'

'So maybe he was calling himself Gonzalez. A lean black-haired man with a foreign accent.'

'Well, if you already knew who it was, why

ask me?' Raggler sounded resentful. His own accent revealed his London origin, east rather than west.

'Confirmation. Why did he want you to follow me?'

'He wanted to know where you was living. He said you'd be going to that house in Fulham and he wanted it watched, continuous.'

'Wasn't that rather a tall order? You couldn't be there all the time.'

'Well, it wouldn't be all the time, would it? I meanter say, there wouldn't be no point in keeping watch all night, would there, Mr Payne?'

'Ah, so you know my name.'

'Yes; he told me.'

'How did he come to engage you?'

'I'm in the Yellow Pages, ain't I? He looked in there and picked me out.'

'Why you?'

'I dunno. Maybe he used a pin.'

Payne thought that if this was so Diaz had had rather poor luck in his choice of investigator. But maybe a seedy character like Raggler suited him better than one of the more reputable agencies.

'Did you see me arrive at the house earlier in the day?'

'Oh yes, I seen you.'

'I didn't notice you then.'

'That's because I was keeping out of sight behind that van what was parked across the road. I kept my head down, but I seen you go in and I seen you come out.'

'But you didn't bother to hide the next time. You just stood there where I could see you. How come?'

'I figured it didn't matter. You'd be going back to your hotel or wherever, and all I had to do was follow. It looked like a real doddle.'

'How did you know you'd got the right man? It might have been a boyfriend and not me at all.'

'He showed me a photo of you, di'n't he?'

Payne did not need to wonder how Diaz had come by a photograph of him. It would have been in the files and he would have had access. It was possible that copies had been issued to the police who had been looking for him before his escape in the yacht *Vagabond*. He had certainly been lucky to get away.

'So after you'd followed me back to base what was supposed to happen then?'

'Nothing. I just report the address to Mr Gonzalez. That's the job completed.'

'Did he tell you why he wanted to find out where I'm staying?'

'No. And I didn't ask. None of my business.'

Payne eased his grip on the private eye. 'A word of advice, Mr Raggler. Pack it in. You could find yourself out of your depth. You could get hurt.'

Raggler was massaging the arm which Payne had released. He flexed it cautiously, as if to make sure there were no bones broken. 'I bin hurt already.'

'Not half as badly as you could be if you don't back off. I don't like people tailing me. And when I take a real dislike to anyone I sometimes get violent. I've just come from a very violent part of the world where a lot of people have been killed. I'm a fighting man, Mr Raggler; it's my trade. So back off, I say. Otherwise you could end up dead. You savvy?'

'You threatening me, Mr Payne?'

'You bet your sweet life I'm threatening you.'

'That's agin the law, you know.'

'So it's against the law. What are you going to do about it?'

'Sometimes,' Raggler said, 'I think this here job just ain't worth the aggro. Straight, I do.'

'Then why don't you give it up? And why don't you start right here and now by getting to hell out of it?'

'What do I tell the client?'

'Tell him you lost me. Tell him I'm living at the Savoy Hotel. Tell him anything you damn well please, but get your feet moving before I give you a boot up the arse.'

Raggler took the hint and got moving. Payne watched him until he was out of sight and then proceeded on his way. This time there was no one following him.

CHAPTER TEN

SEARCH

Payne could see no one keeping watch on Joanna's front door when he called for her the next day. There was no van parked in the street, behind which Raggler could have been hiding, and no one lurking anywhere in the vicinity.

So perhaps he had succeeded in scaring Raggler off. But he doubted whether it would be as easy as that to prevent Diaz from finding out where he was staying. Diaz would not give up at the first setback and he might well switch the search directly to Maria Cardona, employing the same private investigator to trace her whereabouts.

He wondered whether or not to tell Joanna about his encounter with Raggler and finally came to the conclusion that she had a right to know what was going on. She was involved, and maybe she might wish to become uninvolved.

So he told her.

She looked concerned. 'So this Colonel Diaz has brought in some help to find you?'

'Yes.'

'He really means business, doesn't he?'

'I always knew he meant business. This

merely confirms the fact. Does it worry you?'

'A little. I've never had anything to do with this kind of thing before. It's a bit scary, isn't it?'

'You can pull out if you like. I'd understand. I don't want you to do anything you'd really rather not do.'

'But you need my help, don't you?'

'Well, let's put it this way: things would probably be easier for me with you lending a hand, but if you decide to call it a day and fade out I shall just have to manage on my own.'

'And no hard feelings?'

'None at all.'

But regrets, he thought; yes, most certainly regrets. Because, quite apart from the help she was giving, he had to admit that he liked having her around. She was no raving beauty, but she pleased him; he felt at ease in her company; somehow it was as if he had known her for years and wanted to go on knowing her for years to come.

They were in the house and she was moving around, touching things in an absent-minded sort of way, probably thinking over what he had said, thinking about that encounter with Raggler and what he had told her about Diaz, wondering what she might be letting herself in for. Then she stopped what she was doing and said:

'Do you want me to go on helping you?'

'Not if you don't want to. It's up to you.'

'Yes, but forgetting all about my inclinations, do you really want me?'

'Of course I want you,' he said. And he was conscious of a double meaning in the words and wondered whether she was too.

'All right,' she said, 'I'll do it then.'

'You're sure? You're quite sure?'

'Yes, I am. So let's not say any more about it. Let's just get on with the job.'

* * *

Getting on with the job entailed some more of the trawling, visiting again some of the places they had covered the previous day and a few more as well. It was tedious and rather tiring. They had a break for lunch and lingered over it.

'This must be pretty boring for you,' Payne said.

She gave him a swift glance. 'Why do you say that?'

'Well, it's not exactly exciting, is it? All this trailing around from place to place.'

'Do you find it boring?'

'No. But it's different for me, isn't it? I've got nothing better to do.'

'Do you think I have?'

'Well—'

'Don't let it bother you, Alan. If it'll make you feel any better I'll admit that I'm rather enjoying it.'

'You mean that?'

'Don't look so surprised,' she said. 'Of course I mean it. And after all you're paying for the lunch, aren't you?'

* * *

It was early in the evening when they struck gold. It was in a coffee-bar, the kind patronised largely by young people. There was a group of them who looked like students, talking animatedly.

'I know them,' Joanna said; and she made a beeline for the group with Payne in tow.

'Hi, you lot!' she said. 'What's new?'

They all stopped talking and looked at her. They seemed pleased to see her. A pimply young man with a pony tail and a wispy beard said:

'Why, if it isn't Joanna! Where've you been hiding?'

'I haven't been hiding anywhere. I've been around.'

'Not with us, you haven't.'

'Well, no. That's true.'

A plump girl with blonde plaited hair and a headband said: 'Who's the boyfriend?'

'His name's Alan,' Joanna said; and Payne noticed that she did not repudiate the suggestion that he was her boyfriend.

'Hi, Alan!' the girl said. And then to Joanna: 'He's gorgeous. Lucky you.'

Joanna just smiled enigmatically.

A girl with an urchin hair-style and large gold-rimmed glasses asked: 'Seen Maria lately?'

'No,' Joanna said. 'I was going to ask you the same question.'

'The answer's no too.' She looked at the others. 'Any of you seen her?'

There were shakes of the head all round. Apparently no one had.

The pimply young man said: 'Ever since she shacked up with Flash Garry she seems to have been taken out of circulation.'

'You think she's living with him?'

'Seems likely, doesn't it?'

'She fell for him in a big way,' the girl in glasses said. 'Of course it'll all end in tears.'

'You think so.'

'Bound to, isn't it? He's not the type to stick to the same woman for long. There'll be another who'll catch his eye, and Maria won't like that. They'll have an almighty dust-up and she'll be out. She must be crazy.'

The girl in glasses seemed to have it all worked out, Payne thought. He wondered whether there might not be a trace of spite mixed in there. It seemed unlikely that she would be the next one to catch Flash Garry's roving eye.

Joanna told him to get coffee and doughnuts for the whole party, and he carried out the order. They managed to seat themselves with the others and he found himself crushed against the plump girl with the headband. She seemed to have no objection to the close physical contact.

'Tell me about yourself,' she said. 'What do you do?'

Joanna heard the question and answered it for him. 'He's a soldier of fortune.'

'Oh, my goodness!' the plump girl said. 'Is that true? I mean guns and all that?'

'Yes, guns and all that.'

She appeared to be impressed. 'I've never met anyone in that line before.' She put a hand on his arm and squeezed it. 'Tell me more.'

Payne would have liked to escape but there was no possibility of doing so; he was wedged in. The plump girl had him snared and he was obliged to make evasive answers to her gushing interrogation. Meanwhile he could hear Joanna extracting information from the rest of the party.

'Does anyone know where Garry lives?'

The young man with the pony-tail said he had no idea. 'Probably East End. You've heard the way he talks.'

'Now don't be snobby,' the girl in glasses said. 'Just because you don't like him.'

'That has nothing to do with it.'

'Well, if you say so.'

'Why do you want to know where he lives?' the man asked Joanna.

'I'd like to get in touch with Maria. Doesn't

anyone know Garry's address?'

Apparently nobody did. It looked to Payne as if the search for Maria was going to be no further forward than it had been before their arrival at the coffee-bar. Then somebody said:

'Barkingside.'

It was a thin young man wearing a black jacket which looked as if it had been made for someone twice his size; it sagged at the shoulders and the cuffs almost covered his hands. He had said absolutely nothing until now and he seemed embarrassed by drawing attention to himself.

'Barkingside?' Joanna said. 'You mean that's where he lives?'

'Well, yes. His surname is Leeman and he's got a place out there. It's where he does a lot of his business.'

'How do you know all this, Willie?'

Willie seemed to cringe into his jacket. 'I went there once. I bought a motor-bike off him. He said it was a bargain, but it wasn't. It was no good. I had to sell it for scrap.'

The pimply young man with the pony-tail gave him a pitying look. 'You should have known better. Buying a bike off Flash Garry was asking for trouble.'

'I know that now. But I've always thought I'd like a motor-bike and it seemed awfully cheap.'

'Nothing from him is ever really cheap.'

'Well, never mind that now,' Joanna said.

'The thing is you've got his address, have you, Willie?'

'Yes.' He reached inside the voluminous jacket and fished out a small notebook. 'It's in here. I'll write it down for you.' He found the place, tore out a blank page and copied the address on to it with the stub of a pencil. He handed the slip of paper to Joanna.

'Thanks, Willie,' she said. 'You've been a great help.'

He turned quite pink with embarrassment and uttered not another word while Payne and Joanna were there.

*   *   *

They decided not to go out to Barkingside until the next day. It was afternoon when they took to the Underground, and it was a long journey to Barkingside Station on the Central Line, where they eventually left the train. The address given them by the shy young man named Willie was some way from the station and they had to ask to be directed several times before they found it.

It turned out to be an old, rather dilapidated house in an area which looked as if it had suffered from the recession. There were some small factories and other businesses that appeared to have gone under, though others seemed to be managing to ride out the hard times. Leeman's house was reached by way of a narrow lane which appeared to be leading nowhere in particular and it was almost hidden in a large neglected garden that might have been very elegant in the past. Now it had become nothing but a wilderness.

There was a high wall all round it, and a wrought-iron gate was held permanently open by the bindweed and brambles that had become hopelessly entangled with the framework. The drive might once have been gravelled, but there was little of this material in evidence now, and rough grass had taken over except in two parallel tracks worn by the wheels of vehicles.

'So this is it,' Payne said. 'Not exactly a show place, is it?'

'Well, at least it's not overlooked by the neighbours and it probably suits the owner very well. Let's go and see if there's anyone at home.'

They went in through the gateway and up the overgrown drive, and more of the house came into view behind the trees. It was brick-built, probably Victorian, and fairly large. A lot of Virginia creeper had grown up the walls and the tall ground-floor windows came down to lichen-coated stone sills no more than a foot or so high. The dark green paint on the woodwork had a dingy and sombre appearance, and the guttering was in need of repair in places. The roof was slated and there was a porch enclosing the front door.

On the left-hand side of the house the rutted drive continued round to the back, and it was possible to catch a glimpse of decaying outbuildings and some old cars that seemed to have been dumped there. No sign of human life was visible about the place; overall it had a depressingly abandoned and deserted appearance.

'I just hope there is somebody at home,' Joanna said. 'Otherwise we've come a long way for nothing.'

'Well, we'll soon find out.'

They walked up to the front door, a massive piece of oak with a tarnished brass knob and an iron knocker made in the shape of a wreath. There had apparently once been a bell-pull on the right, but it had become weakened with rust and had broken away, leaving the lower part hanging in the guides but joined to nothing above. So it had to be the knocker, and Payne gave a smart rat-tat-tat with it, which scared some pigeons out of the ivy-clad trees. They flew away with a noisy flapping of wings and disappeared.

Payne and Joanna waited in the porch and nothing happened. There was not a sound coming from inside the house and it began to seem likely that there was indeed no one at home.

'Give it another go,' Joanna suggested.

He did so. Still nobody came to open the door.

'Looks as if it's an empty house.'

'I suppose we should have expected this.' Joanna sounded depressed. 'But somehow it never occurred to me that they might not be here. Do we wait or do we go away and come back later?'

'Let's do some nosing around first. Might find something of interest at the back.'

What they found were the old cars and some sheds full of all kinds of junk, the grass and weeds rampant everywhere. Beyond the sheds was what might once have been a delightful walled garden extending to about half an acre. There were gnarled old apple and pear trees, a decayed greenhouse that was nothing but a mass of rotting wood and broken glass, beds edged with box which had grown into unkempt hedges, and at the far end a rustic summer-house with a roof of moulting thatch. In the summer-house a woman was sitting on a rickety wicker chair reading a book.

She glanced up in surprise when she heard them coming. She was young and quite a beauty; black-haired, sloe-eyed, fine-boned. Payne's first thought on seeing her was that she must have inherited her looks from the mother he had never seen, for there was nothing about her that reminded him in the least of the late President Cardona.

Joanna gave a cry of delight. 'Maria!'

The other girl got up from her chair, the book in one hand, and appeared uncertain how to respond to the greeting. She was not as tall as Joanna, but she was slender and there was no impression of dumpiness about her. Payne could see why Garry Leeman, or any other man, would be attracted to her, quite apart from any considerations of financial gain. She was casually dressed in a white sweater and jeans and a pair of rather scuffed suede shoes with flat heels, but this did nothing to detract from her charm. She still looked lovely.

Joanna, after a momentary hesitation, ran to her and embraced her. This again seemed to startle her, but she made no effort to avoid the embrace and rather appeared to welcome it.

'I'm so glad to see you again,' Joanna said. 'Forget and forgive?'

'There's nothing to forgive,' Maria assured her. 'We both lost our heads a little, I think. I've been longing to see you, too.'

Payne felt like the odd one out in this mutual reconciliation, which was apparently so welcome to both the girls. He stood a few yards away from them and waited patiently to be brought into the picture.

It was Joanna who suddenly remembered he was there. 'Oh dear,' she said, 'I'm forgetting to introduce Alan. Alan Payne. I don't think you two have met.'

Maria looked at him. 'No; I'm sure we haven't, have we, Mr Payne?'

'No,' Payne said, 'we haven't. You had left the Presidential Palace before I arrived there.'

Once again she was startled; he could see that. 'I don't understand. You have been there?'

'Yes. I was employed by your father.'

'Oh!'

He felt slightly embarrassed, not knowing whether or not she had heard of Cardona's death. It was possible that the news had not reached her here, unlikely as that might seem.

'You know he's—'

'Dead?' she said. 'Yes, I know.' She spoke without emotion. It was as she might have reacted to the mention of the death of a perfect stranger, as though it meant nothing to her. Then she asked with some curiosity: 'In what way were you employed by him?'

'He's a mercenary,' Joanna said. She turned to him for confirmation, a trifle mockingly, he thought, as though she were teasing him. 'Aren't you, Alan?'

'If that's what you insist on calling it.'

Maria regarded him coldly, and he could tell that he had plummeted in her estimation. 'So you were fighting for him?'

'Not exactly. My job was to advise on military matters and instruct the Palace Guard.'

'I see. You let other people do the fighting for you.'

'Not for me. For the President.'

'Oh, of course. But I still don't quite understand. Were you in the palace at the time of the final battle?'

'Yes.'

'So how did you get away?'

'By crossing the river from the back of the building under cover of darkness.'

'Ah, you escaped before the palace fell. That was clever of you.' She spoke sarcastically. 'To save your own skin. You did not consider that you had been paid to die for a lost cause?'

Payne answered calmly, refusing to be goaded into a heated retort. 'The question didn't arise. I was ordered to leave by the President himself.'

This appeared to astonish her. 'Indeed! Why?'

'There was a job he wanted me to do.'

'What kind of job?'

'He wished me to act as his courier. That is why I am here. He gave me your address in Fulham, but of course he didn't know you had moved your quarters.'

Maria glanced at Joanna as if for enlightenment.

'He came to the house,' Joanna said. 'I agreed to help him find you. It wasn't easy. You'd just disappeared and I didn't know where you'd gone.'

Maria spoke to Payne. 'You say my father wanted you to act as his courier and he sent you to me?'

'Yes.'

'With a letter?'

'No, not a letter. A gift. The last he would ever send you.'

She made a gesture of repudiation. 'I want no gift from him. He should have known I would not accept it. He knew I had renounced everything he stood for and wanted no more to do with him.'

'You have not yet heard what the gift is.'

'I do not wish to hear. It is enough that it comes from him.'

'All the same perhaps you should let me tell you what it is before you reject it out of hand.'

'I cannot prevent you telling me,' she said, 'but I assure you it will make no difference.'

'Not even if it were to be a diamond of great value?'

She stared at him. 'You are surely not speaking of the Emperor Stone?'

'I believe that is what it has been called.'

'A diamond!' Joanna cried. 'So that's what this something of great value is! You didn't tell me.'

'Well, I've told you now,' Payne said.

Maria still seemed to be trying to get to grips with the significance of what he had revealed. 'But if it is that, it is worth an enormous amount.'

'Half a million dollars at least, so I've been told. Possibly much more. Are you still determined to refuse it?'

'Even more so than before. My father had no right to give it away; it was never legally his.'

'So you will not take it?'

She answered firmly: 'No.'

'Well,' Payne said, 'this puts me in a rather difficult position. What am I to do with it?'

'You have not thought of taking it for yourself?'

'I have thought of it and rejected the idea. Why else would I be here?'

'Even though you are a mercenary, a soldier of fortune?'

'A soldier of fortune is not necessarily without scruples.'

'So you are an honest man?'

'Do you find that so unbelievable?'

She seemed to relent a little towards him. 'Forgive me. Perhaps I am becoming over-suspicious. And I am forgetting my manners. Won't the two of you come indoors. I will make some tea and we can talk.'

She led the way back to the house through the jungle of a garden. They went in by the back door, which opened into a large kitchen, only partly modernised. Here she made tea in a china pot, found a tin of biscuits in one of the cupboards, loaded everything on to a tray and conducted them to a sitting-room in another part of the house. This was furnished haphazardly with a sofa and a few armchairs, various other items that might have made up some of the stock of an antiques shop, nothing matching, and a lot of expensive high-fi equipment on one side. The ceiling was lofty, rather smoke-blackened, and there was a rusty iron grate in front of which was standing an incongruous-looking electric fire.

Maria had just finished pouring the tea and they were all sitting down when the sound of a car driving up to the house could be heard. It went round to the back and a door slammed.

'Oh dear!' Maria said. 'That must be Garry. I wasn't expecting him back quite so soon.'

Payne got the impression that she was nervous. He wondered why. There seemed to be no reason for it.

She put down her cup and got to her feet. 'I'll go and tell him we're in here.' Rather hurriedly she left the room.

Payne said: 'She's a bit jumpy, isn't she? Am I wrong in having the feeling that she wasn't too happy to have him back just yet?'

'I have the same feeling,' Joanna said.

'Can you think of any reason?'

'At a guess,' she said, 'I'd say she's expecting to have an argument with him and isn't too happy about it.'

'An argument over what?'

'Isn't it obvious?' The diamond, of course.'

'Ah! I see.'

CHAPTER ELEVEN

PROBLEM

When the door opened again and Maria came in with the man Payne had his first sight of Garry Leeman, and he had to admit that this was the kind of male who had the physical attributes to captivate any reasonably susceptible female of the species; and never mind what his character was like.

'So,' Leeman said, 'we have visitors. Unexpected too. Hello, Joanna. So you decided to come and make it up with Maria. Have you pardoned her for taking up with a snake like yours truly?'

He spoke banteringly. He was probably getting on for thirty years old, slim, about six feet tall and black-haired, having the rather sinister good looks of an old-time stage villain. He was dressed in easy-fitting clothes that had an expensive look about them, and it was obvious that he cared about his appearance.

'Well,' Joanna said, 'it was you who used the word.' Which did not really answer the question.

Leeman glanced at Payne. 'I don't think we've met before.'

'We haven't,' Payne said. And he was thinking that he could have gone on managing very well without the acquaintance of Garry Leeman. There were persons you took an instant dislike to, and for him this was one of them. And it would have been just the same if Joanna had not already blackened Leeman's character; that merely served to confirm his own immediate impression that he was a louse.

'I'm Payne.'

'Not a pain in the neck, I hope,' Leeman said, with a laugh at his own wit.

Nobody else joined in the laughter. Joanna frowned. Maria looked embarrassed.

Leeman was not in the least put out by this lack of appreciation. 'So,' he said, 'do I get a cuppa or don't I? There's enough in the old pot, I suppose. Or have you lot guzzled it all?'

Maria said hurriedly: 'No, there's plenty. I'll fetch another cup. Just a moment.'

She went out of the room and Leeman flopped down in an armchair and stretched out his legs. He was wearing the kind of shoes that Payne would not have been seen dead in: blue slip-ons with toggles and interwoven uppers like basketwork in leather.

'So, Joanna,' Leeman said, 'how's life been treating you?'

'It hasn't. I've had to pay for myself.'

Leeman grinned, displaying a set of perfect teeth, whose gleaming whiteness contrasted with the neatly-trimmed black moustache above.

'Out of a job, eh?'

'Yes, out of a job.'

'There's a lot of it about. Maybe you should come and work for me.'

'Even if that were a serious offer,' she said, 'I still wouldn't consider it for a moment.'

'Still got a grudge against me, have you? Oh well, I'll just have to grin and bear it.'

Maria came back with the extra cup and filled it for him. He took the cup and added three teaspoonfuls of sugar from the bowl she held for him. He stirred the tea and turned to Payne.

'So what line are you in, Mr Payne?'

'None at present.'

'Like that, is it? Another on the dole queue.'

'Not that either. I've only been back in England a few days.'

'Been working abroad, have you?'

'Yes.'

'What part of the world?'

'Central America.'

'That a fact? Now there's a coincidence. Maria comes from down that way.'

'Not so much of a coincidence,' Payne said. 'That's why I'm here.'

It was obvious that Leeman was interested now. What had started as merely an exchange of small-talk had developed into something more, and he was quick to pick up the scent of a piece of business that might turn out to be to his advantage.

'You'd better explain that. Sounds

interesting.'

Maria broke in swiftly. 'It's nothing important, Garry. Nothing for you to be concerned about.' It was evident to Payne that she did not want him to know about the diamond.

But Leeman was having nothing of that. 'Anything that concerns you, sweetheart, has to concern me too. It follows. Tell me, Mr Payne—Oh, sod it, I can't go on calling you mister. What's your first name?'

'Alan.'

'Well, tell me, Alan; why are you here just because you happened to be working in the country Maria comes from?'

'I'm on a mission from her father.'

'President Cardona! But he's dead, ain't he? The other lot took over and snuffed him out. That's the way I heard it.'

'You heard right. But he was still alive when I left.'

'I see. And what's this mission you're talking about?'

Payne glanced at Maria, an eyebrow lifting in question. She gave a shrug, apparently resigned to having Leeman told.

'I've brought a gift from him,' Payne said. 'A farewell gift, you might call it. He knew he was going to die.'

'Aha!' A gleam had come into Leeman's eye, a gleam of cupidity. 'So what's this gift, then?'

Again Payne glanced questioningly at the

145

girl. Again she made that shrug of resignation which gave him leave to reveal everything.

'It's a diamond.'

The gleam in Leeman's eye became more pronounced. 'A diamond, is it? Now I don't suppose when you say a diamond you mean an itsy-bitsy little stone like you'd get in any old tuppenny-ha'penny ring. Coming from a man like him, it's gotta be something pretty big, ain't it? Is it big? Real big?'

'Yes, it's big.'

'Worth about how much, would you say?'

This time Payne did not bother to glance at Maria. 'I can't give a precise figure, but I have been told that half a million dollars would be much below the mark.'

Leeman whistled softly. 'Half a million bucks! Now that's real money in anybody's language.' He looked at Maria. 'Sweetheart, you're an heiress. You're rich.'

'I have refused to take it,' she said.

Leeman stared at her as if unable to believe that he had heard correctly. 'You have what?'

She repeated the simple statement. 'I have refused to take it.'

'Well, for Christ's sake! Why?'

'For many reasons. In the first place it was not his to give. He stole it.'

'Stole it! From who?'

'From the people of my country. It was part of the palace treasure. The most valuable of all the jewels.'

'So what! He was president, wasn't he? He could do what he liked with the treasure.'

'Only because he had the power, which he had seized for himself. He had never been elected by a popular vote.'

'Well, I don't know nothing about that. And anyways, it's neither here nor there. The point is he sent the diamond to you before he died and there's no damned reason in the world why you shouldn't take it.'

'There is every reason,' she said.

'Now look here, sweetheart,' Leeman was beginning to lose his temper. 'You're acting like a stupid bloody idiot. You're making this grand gesture and throwing away a fortune. Well, that's all fine and dandy; it may make you feel good; but what about me? Have you given one tiny little thought to how this affects G. Leeman Esquire?'

'I don't understand,' Maria said, frowning slightly.

And that, Payne thought, put her in a minority of one. Because it was a dead cert that the other three people in the room understood perfectly well that Leeman was thinking about his own share of the fortune and was appalled at the very idea of not grabbing it with both hands.

'You don't understand?' he said. 'What are you? Some kinda nut-case? What are you aiming to live on from here on in? There'll be nothing more coming from the old man, that's for sure. Of course you'll say you wouldn't have taken it if there was, but that's just a load of crap. You ever tried being a pauper? It ain't much fun, believe you me. So what you been meaning to do? Live off me?'

She said nothing. She just looked at him in a hurt sort of way, as though a side of his character to which she had previously been blind were now being revealed to her without disguise. And he did not spare her; he went on spelling it out so that there could be no mistake.

'It ain't on, you know. I ain't made of money. I have to work hard for what I get. I've never had it easy like what you have; I've had to graft from the time when I was a kid, using my wits and keeping an eye open to the main chance. And now along comes something for nothing, a windfall if ever there was one, and you say: "No thanks. Take it away. I don't want it." Well, I want it. You bet your sweet life I do. And I don't give a damn about how your old man come by it, and that's the truth.'

She understood now. It was impossible not to understand. It could not have been more plainly spelt out to her.

'So,' she said, 'what you are saying is that if I do not accept this gift you will turn me out?'

'Well, sweetheart, it's up to you.'

'I thought you loved me.' She spoke sadly but without passion, as if quietly disillusioned. Perhaps she was not even greatly surprised.

She had been living with him long enough to gain some insight into his motives. But perhaps she had refused to believe the evidence presented to her; had not wished to believe it.

He gave a contemptuous laugh. 'Love! Oh dear, oh dear! That's a proper load of old cobblers. It don't pay the rent, you know.' Suddenly a new idea seemed to come into his head and he turned to Payne. 'Let's have a dekko.'

'Come again?'

'The sparkler. Let's have a butcher's at it.'

'You can't,' Payne said. 'I haven't got it with me.'

'Haven't got it with you! But I thought you came here to give it to Maria.'

'No, I came to tell her about it. I couldn't be certain we'd find her. You don't imagine I carry a thing like that around in my pocket, do you?'

'So where is it?'

'In a safe place.'

Leeman spoke to Joanna. 'Have you seen it?'

'No. Until a short while ago I didn't even know what it was. Alan simply told me it was something valuable.'

Leeman turned his suspicious eyes on Payne. 'You ain't dishing out a lot of bullshit, are you? I mean, this ain't some stupid game you're playing, is it?'

'Now what do you think?'

'Of course it's not a game,' Maria said. 'How

would he have known about the Emperor Stone if he wasn't genuine?'

'What in hell's the Emperor Stone?'

'It's the name of the diamond.'

'Oh, so it's got a name, has it? Well, well!'

'And besides,' Payne said, 'what would I stand to gain by coming here with such a story if it were not true? I know better ways of spending my time.'

'So what's in it for you?'

'I've already been paid for my services.'

'But not half a million?'

'No, nothing like that.'

'Old man Cardona must've had a lot of trust in you.' Leeman spoke with a kind of wonder, approaching disbelief. 'I meanter say, what was to prevent you taking the sparkler for yourself?'

'Is that what you would have done in my place?'

'Now, now,' Leeman said. 'Let's not get personal.'

Which was pretty rich coming from him, Payne thought.

'And now,' he said, 'we have a problem, don't we?'

'What problem. I don't see none. You go and pick up the goody and bring it here. That'll be your job done.'

'But suppose when I bring it Miss Cardona won't accept the stone? Suppose she still refuses to have anything to do with it? What then?'

'Then you just leave it here and beat it. You'll have carried out your orders. After that you can leave the worrying to me.'

'I don't think I can do that.'

'Why not?'

'Well, the way I see it is this. If Miss Cardona won't accept the gift and I just dump it here and wash my hands of the whole business, who's likely to pick it up? I give you one guess.'

Leeman's face reddened and he spoke angrily. 'She'll pick it up herself. After we've had a little heart-to-heart talk I guarantee she'll change her mind. Don't you bother yourself about that.'

'But I do bother about it. It's my responsibility, don't you see?'

'All I see is you're thinking of hanging on to it yourself, and never mind all the fine talk about responsibility and that. Her saying she won't take it just gives you the excuse you're looking for, don't it?'

Payne did not bother to deny the charge; it seemed pointless. He spoke to Maria. 'Do you think you'll change your mind?'

She answered without hesitation: 'No.'

'All right,' Leeman said. 'So you don't want it. So why don't you give it to me? That would make it all legal and above board.' He turned to Payne. 'That's okay, ain't it? I mean it's hers to do what she likes with. She can do any damn thing she pleases with it, can't she?'

'I suppose so,' Payne admitted with some reluctance. 'Do you want to give it to him, Maria?'

Again she answered firmly: 'No.'

It seemed to madden Leeman. He began to shout at her. 'You stupid bitch! You need your head seeing to.' He jumped up and made a move as if to attack her, but Payne quickly intercepted him and took a restraining grip on his arm.

'Cool it, Garry.'

'Lemme go, can't you?' Leeman was still furious. 'I'll knock some sense into that bloody head of hers, see if I don't.'

'No, you won't. You'll sit down and behave yourself.' Payne forced him back into the armchair. 'You won't gain anything by violence.'

Leeman seemed to come to the conclusion that this was true, and he gave way, though obviously still incensed by what he evidently regarded as the girl's unreasonable obstinacy. She, for her part, remained admirably calm, though there could be no doubt that she was distressed by his behaviour, which betrayed the naked greed that motivated him. Perhaps already she was falling out of love with him and regretting the impetuosity that had persuaded her to throw in her lot with such a man.

Payne spoke to her again. 'Now let's try to work something out. Since you refuse to accept the diamond, what do you suggest I should do with it?'

'It should be taken back to where it belongs.'

'To your country?'

'Of course.'

'And are you suggesting that I should take it?'

'Why not? You were the one who brought it to England.'

'True. But you must realise that I would almost certainly be arrested the moment I set foot in the country and might even end up hanging from a rope or stood up in front of a firing-squad. It's not a prospect that appeals to me very much, I must admit.'

'You could send it.'

'By post? I think that would be a very dodgy method. Who would I address it to?'

She said nothing to that. She seemed to be stumped and was not looking at all happy.

'I don't think any of us should be too hasty about this,' Payne said. 'It might not be a bad idea if we were to take time to think things over. I suggest we sleep on it. Suppose I come back tomorrow and see whether you're in the same frame of mind. What do you say?'

'I have told you my decision has been made.'

'Yes, but it's my experience that second thoughts have a way of coming up after a time. I think we should at least take a chance on it. So how about it?'

She agreed somewhat reluctantly. 'If you wish. But I assure you it will make no difference.'

Leeman looked as if he would have liked to raise objections but could think of no convincing reason for doing so. All he said was: 'I just hope you don't get other ideas yourself and decide not to come back. Where are you staying?'

'I don't think that's any of your business,' Payne said.

'How'd you get here? I didn't see no car.'

'I haven't got one. We came by tube.'

'Oh gawd! And you mean to come that way tomorrow?'

'Yes. Why not?'

'People get mugged on the tube. Suppose you was to be. Suppose some mugger took the diamond off you. Have you thought of that?'

'I've brought it a long way and I haven't lost it yet. I don't think any tinpot mugger is going to take it from me now.'

'But you can't be sure, can you? How would it be if I was to come for you in my car? Save a lot of bother.'

Payne could see how it was: Leeman did not trust him to return the next day and thought he could lessen the risk by providing the transport. He just could not wait to get his sticky fingers on the gem. But that was not at all the way Payne had planned things. He had not put his life at risk simply to benefit a bastard like this.

'I don't mind the bother,' he said. 'And I

prefer the tube. I don't know what sort of driver you are, do I? I wouldn't want to end up as a road accident statistic.'

Leeman scowled, perhaps resenting the slur on his driving ability. People tended to be sensitive in that respect.

Payne stood up. 'Tomorrow then. About the same time. Okay?'

Leeman shrugged. 'I suppose so.'

Maria said nothing. She seemed unhappy about the whole business.

*   *   *

As he and Joanna were walking away from the entrance to Leeman's place Payne noticed a car parked at the side of the road about twenty yards from the gateway. It was a not very new black Fiat, rather mud-bespattered and neglected in appearance. A man was sitting behind the wheel, slumped down with his chin almost on his chest and a hat pulled over his forehead, so that it was difficult to see much of his face through the grimy windscreen.

He did not glance up when the two of them walked past, but the tweed hat put Payne in mind of a man named Raggler who had also worn just such a hat. Raggler had worn a blue trenchcoat and this man had no coat on, but it could have been in the back of the car. So could this be Raggler, still doing his tailing job even though he had been warned off? Payne could not be sure; the glimpse he had caught of the half-obscured face had not been enough to tell him for certain one way or the other; but he had a feeling that it was indeed the private eye.

Yet all the evidence was against it. How could the man possibly have followed them in a car when they had travelled down by the Underground Railway? It just did not make sense. So it had to be someone else. After all, a tweed hat was hardly sufficient identification; they were not such an uncommon form of headgear.

'No, it couldn't have been.'

He was hardly aware that he had spoken the words aloud until his companion gave him a questioning glance and said: 'What couldn't have been?'

'There was a man in that parked car. I thought it might have been Raggler.'

'You mean the man who followed you yesterday?'

'Yes.'

'But that's hardly likely, is it? He couldn't have trailed us all the way here. In a car, I mean. Did you recognise him?'

'No. I didn't get a good enough view of his face. But I had the impression that he didn't want me to. He'd got his head down and the hat pulled over his eyes.'

'You must have been imagining things. Maybe he was asleep.'

'Yes, maybe he was.'

'There's really no way it could have been Raggler, is there?'

'No, I don't suppose there is,' Payne said.

But the feeling was still there. All reason told him that the man in the black Fiat had not been the seedy private investigator, and yet he could not free himself of the suspicion that it had been.

It worried him a little.

CHAPTER TWELVE

ARGUMENT

He called for her again the next morning. He had suggested that perhaps she might not wish to have anything more to do with the business now that Maria had been located.

'You've been a great help, but if you'd prefer to bow out now I can manage on my own from here.'

'Are you telling me you don't want my company any more?'

'No. I love having your company. I just thought you might be getting fed up with tagging along with me.'

'For your information,' she said, 'I rather like tagging along with you. I haven't much else to do, have I?'

It might have been more flattering, he

thought, if she had omitted the final sentence; but he let it go.

When he called for her he could see no one hanging around who might be keeping watch on the place; they seemed to have given up that ploy. He thought again of the man in the black Fiat and wondered whether it could possibly have been Raggler, but again he came to the conclusion that it was far too unlikely. He half regretted now that he had not made certain at the time; he could have tapped on the window of the car and made the man look at him; but it was too late to think about that now.

They did not go out to Barkingside until late in the day, even though he had told Leeman it would be earlier. The weather was good and they strolled around sight-seeing like a couple of ordinary tourists. They saw the Tower and Westminster Abbey and had lunch in Soho, and time slipped away unheeded.

'You know,' she said, 'I've lived in London for years and there's loads of it I've never seen. Silly, isn't it?'

'If you like we could see a lot more of it when this other matter is settled; really spend some time on it. Does the idea appeal to you at all?'

'It appeals to me very much. Yes, let's do that.'

But the other matter was still unconcluded, and it had to be attended to. Yet, because of the dallying, it was evening before they arrived at Barkingside, and they walked to Leeman's place through the gathering dusk.

There was no black Fiat parked near the entrance, and Payne remarked on this.

'Did you imagine there would be?' Joanna asked.

'Not really. It was just a thought.'

'People don't spend all their time sitting in cars, you know.'

'No. It just seems like it.'

There were lights on in the house, yet somehow it still had a dark and oddly sinister appearance. Perhaps it was the jungle surrounding it that contributed to this effect.

'Well,' Payne said, 'at least it looks as if somebody is at home.'

'I don't think there was much likelihood that there wouldn't be. Garry is probably out of his mind with impatience.'

As if to confirm this suggestion, it was he who opened the door to them only a second or two after Payne had used the knocker.

'So here you are,' he said. 'I thought you were never coming. You took your bloody time.'

He sounded resentful. He had probably been waiting on tenterhooks for their arrival and getting more and more steamed up as the hours passed. But there was more to it than that; he appeared to be nervous, on edge; he just could not keep still. It could have been the thought of seeing the diamond, of holding it in his hand, that was affecting him and making the excitement difficult to contain.

'Well, come on in,' he said. 'Don't just stand there. Come inside, for God's sake.'

They went in and he shut the door, slammed it, as if his haste would not allow him to close it gently.

'This way.'

He shepherded them into the room where they had taken tea the previous day. The lights were on in there and curtains were drawn across the windows. Maria was sitting in one of the armchairs, looking unhappy. She had reason to be, because she was not alone; there were two other people in the room. One was the seedy private eye, Raggler, and the other was Colonel Bernardo Diaz.

'Ah!' Diaz said. 'So you have come at last.' And he gave a grin, baring his teeth like a wolf.

Both men were sitting down, but Raggler for one seemed far from relaxed; he looked uneasy, like someone who had got himself caught up in a situation he was not at all sure he could manage. He was not wearing the tweed hat now, and there was a bald patch visible on the crown of his head. He was not wearing the trenchcoat either; he was in a crumpled charcoal-grey suit and a horrible yellow slipover with holes in it. Everything about him gave the inescapable impression that he was not finding much of a gold-mine in the private investigation racket.

Diaz, in contrast, looked very dapper in a

dark blue suit and a white shirt and silk tie. His hair and moustache were neatly trimmed, but his cheeks and chin were shadowed by a hint of stubble. He had probably shaved that morning, but his was the kind of face that needed two shaves a day. He seemed perfectly at ease, a man who had everything under control. He was seated in another of the armchairs, strategically positioned facing the doorway, and his right elbow was resting on the arm. In the hand was a medium-sized self-loading pistol which was pointing in the direction of the newcomers.

'Close the door, Mr Leeman,' Diaz said.

Leeman did so, and promptly moved out of the possible line of fire, leaving Payne and Joanna standing where they had come to a halt just inside the room.

Payne looked at Raggler. 'So it really was you I saw in the car yesterday. I had a feeling it might be.'

Raggler gave a kind of wriggle, but said nothing.

'You didn't take my advice. Naughty of you.'

'Mr Raggler believes in doing what is best for his client,' Diaz said. 'He reported to me the encounter with you, when you threatened to break his arm. And then you threatened that even worse things could happen to him if he didn't stop working for me.'

'But he still is.'

'Yes. We put our heads together and decided there might be a better way than following you. We came to the conclusion that as your intention was to deliver the article to Maria Cardona it would serve our purpose if we switched the hunt to her. So Mr Raggler made inquiries and discovered that she was living with a Mr Garry Leeman; and after that it took him no time at all to run Mr Leeman to earth.'

'Clever Mr Raggler,' Payne said. It was evident to him now that the man was not such a slouch at his job as his appearance might have suggested. He had made quick work of tracing Maria. 'So you took him into your confidence? You told him what it was all about?'

'It seemed advisable.'

'So what's he paying you, Raggler?' Payne asked. 'Now that you know what the score is I guess the fee's gone up, hasn't it?'

Raggler did another wriggle. 'The price of my services is confidential. It is no concern of anyone except me and Mr Gonzalez.'

'Ah, come off it, Raggler. Stop calling him Gonzalez. His name's Diaz. Ask Miss Cardona if you don't believe me.'

'The name is immaterial. The client is entitled to call himself whatever he chooses.'

'Sure he is. But don't you think you're taking one hell of a risk working for him? The fee will need to be a mighty big one to compensate you for being party to a felony.'

'Felony! Who's talking about any felony? As

I understand it, the article belongs to Mr Gonzalez's government. When he has gained possession of it he will return it to them.'

'And that's how you understand it?' Payne shook his head in mock admonishment. 'Raggler, you really are a dreadful liar. You weren't born yesterday and you know as well as I do that Mr Diaz has no intention of restoring the diamond—let's call it what we all know it is—to anyone, government or not. He means to keep it for himself.'

'I don't know that,' Raggler said.

'You mean you don't want to know it. You prefer to turn a blind eye to the truth of the matter.'

Diaz broke in then. 'It makes no difference what Mr Raggler knows or does not know. We are wasting time. I take it, Payne, that you have brought the diamond?'

'Then you take it wrong. I haven't.'

Diaz frowned. 'What nonsense is this?' He turned to Leeman. 'You said he would be bringing it. That is what you said, is it not?'

Leeman answered sulkily: 'It's what he told us he'd do.'

'No, Garry, that's not true, and you know it isn't,' Payne said. 'All I promised was that I'd come again to see whether Maria had changed her mind about taking it. I didn't say I'd bring it.'

'It's what you implied.'

'Correction. It's what you thought I implied,

and that's quite a different kettle of fish. But what's all this about you telling Mr Diaz? Why did you have to tell him anything?'

'Because he threatened to shoot me if I didn't, that's why. You think I wanter get my head blown off?'

'It might not be a bad idea at that.' It was apparent to Payne that Leeman was a lot less tough than he would have liked to give the impression of being. Under threats from Diaz he had soon caved in and given the colonel all the information he required. 'When did this happen?'

'This morning. Him and the other guy, they turned up here and walked straight in without a by-your-leave nor nothing. They thought the diamond would be here. Took some convincing you hadn't brought it yesterday when they knew you was here.'

Payne could believe that. Raggler would have reported to Diaz the visit of the previous day, and the only surprising thing was that he had not made his move that evening. But perhaps Raggler had left it until the morning before making his report; there would not have been as much urgency in his mind as in Diaz's. And so they had been waiting here for most of the day; he could well imagine with what impatience.

Diaz had allowed Leeman to make his explanation without interruption, but now he broke in again.

'Why didn't you bring the diamond?'

'Because,' Payne said, 'as I explained to this gentleman yesterday, I don't fancy going around with something as valuable as that in my pocket.'

'But you were going to give it to Miss Cardona.'

'Only if she had changed her mind and was willing to take it. If she had, I could have gone back for it or she could have come with me and picked it up.' He turned to Maria. 'Have you changed your mind?'

She spoke for the first time, her voice low but firm. 'No. I still do not wish to have it.'

'Let us have an end to this nonsense,' Diaz snapped. 'Whether she would be willing to accept or not is completely irrelevant now. I am going to take it, and that is that.'

'Do you want Colonel Diaz to have it, Maria?' Payne asked. 'It's for you to say.'

'Only if his intention is to return it to the people to whom it rightly belongs.'

'So, Colonel,' Payne said, 'you have heard what the lady insists on. Do you intend to do that?'

Diaz answered without hesitation: 'Of course. That is my sole purpose. I am here as the representative of the new government. My mission is to recover the stone, which is not only valuable in itself but is also a part of my country's national heritage.'

It was a fine little speech, smoothly

delivered, and the words were persuasive. But Payne had no doubt at all that the man was lying. He would have said anything that might help him to gain possession of the diamond.

Payne spoke again to Maria. 'Do you believe this?'

She looked doubtful. 'I don't know what to believe. What do you think?'

'I think there is something you should remember. Colonel Diaz was one of the leading figures in the junta headed by your father. It now transpires that he was a traitor, in cahoots with the enemy. He slipped away before the final defeat, and I saw him riding in a Mercedes with an officer of the revolutionary army, apparently on very friendly terms with him.'

Diaz seemed to be a trifle startled by this revelation, but he was far from being disconcerted. 'This only goes to prove that I am a genuine envoy of the new regime and that what I have told you is true.'

'It also proves that you were a traitor to the Cardona government; and a man who has acted treacherously once may well do so again. Have you any proof that you are acting on behalf of the new regime?'

'What proof should I have?'

'A written warrant, perhaps? Some official document that would convince a sceptic like me that you haven't been feeding us a pack of lies and that you don't intend to grab the Emperor Stone just for yourself. Show us something, Colonel, so that we may know you are not as corrupt as I believe you are.'

Diaz's face reddened with passion. 'I will show you nothing. Who are you to demand such a thing of me? Who are you to doubt my word? A soldier of fortune, who is no doubt intending to take the jewel for his own ends.'

Payne smiled. 'Now really, Colonel, you shouldn't get so heated. Then you might not make such a ridiculous accusation. If I had wished to keep the diamond, would I have bothered to bring it so far and offer it to Miss Cardona? I could have gone straight to Amsterdam and sold it. Which is perhaps what you are intending to do.'

Diaz seemed to be choking with rage and could not get a word out. He glowered at Payne with hatred, fingers gripping the pistol so hard that the knuckles showed white. Payne had little doubt that the colonel would dearly have loved to shoot him and was only restrained by the thought that by doing so he might be saying goodbye to any chance of getting the diamond.

Payne ignored him. 'Well, Maria, you see how it is. I leave it to you to judge whether Colonel Diaz is as altruistic as he would have you believe. Do you wish to entrust the Emperor Stone to him? Do you think he would restore it to your people?'

'No,' she said. 'I do not.'

This answer seemed to be the last straw for Diaz. He leaped up from his chair in a fury, rushed to where the girl was sitting and struck her on the face with the palm of his hand. The blow rocked her to one side, but she had a temper of her own and she jumped up and slapped Diaz on the cheek in return. Payne had not seen her roused before, and he had imagined her to be of a very equable temperament. And perhaps in normal circumstances she was, but being slapped by a man like Diaz was hardly normal and it had been enough to draw from her a swift reaction.

The tit-for-tat blow had been delivered with considerable energy, and must have stung Diaz. He had not been expecting it, and it inflamed him all the more, so that he struck the girl again, but this time with his clenched fist. She gave a cry of pain and fell back on to the chair in which she had been sitting, blood starting almost immediately to flow from a cut lip. Diaz appeared ready to punish her further, and might have done so if Payne had not intervened. He reached Diaz in three strides and laid a hand none too lightly on his shoulder and swung him round.

'That's enough.'

This interference did nothing to moderate Diaz's fury. Indeed, it served only to madden him even more. He had delivered his blows with the left hand, but he still had the pistol in the other one, and now he brought it up and pressed the trigger.

It was a wild shot, the reflex action of a man

who had for the moment lost all control of himself. The crack of the gun set Payne's ears ringing, but the bullet flew past and buried itself in the wall behind him, not a foot from where Leeman was standing. This brave character gave a yelp of fright and dropped to the floor as if he had in fact been shot.

Payne hit Diaz on the side of the jaw and knocked him down. He was about to follow up with some more of the treatment, but Diaz, though down, was far from out; he was still holding the pistol and from the prone position he quickly brought it to bear on his assailant.

'Stop!'

Payne stopped. He believed it was touch and go whether Diaz would fire again, but it was more likely that he would if he were attacked; and he might not miss the target a second time.

Raggler's voice now broke in. 'Mr Gonzalez! Mr Gonzalez! Please!' He seemed appalled by what had happened and maybe feared that worse might follow.

Diaz snarled at him: 'Don't call me that. It's not my name. You know that now.'

Raggler cringed. 'I beg your pardon. But Mr Diaz, think. Don't do anything rash.'

Diaz was getting to his feet. Payne could see that the immediate danger had passed and that he was in control of himself again. In his fit of passion he might have killed; he was not the man to have much respect for the sanctity of human life; but as soon as the fit had subsided he would see that it was not to his advantage to eliminate the man who was possibly the only person who knew where the diamond was.

He fingered his jaw, which could have been paining him, and glared at the man who had inflicted the damage. 'I shall remember this.'

'Good,' Payne said.

'Not so good for you perhaps. You may come to regret striking me in this way.'

'Well, we shall have to wait and see about that. You shouldn't have hit Miss Cardona. Don't you know it's very ungentlemanly to do a thing like that? But perhaps you are not a gentleman.'

Joanna had gone to Maria and was dabbing at her cut lip with a handkerchief. She glanced at Diaz with contempt.

'You are a pig.'

He seemed inclined to hit her too, but contented himself with an insult. 'And you are a whore.'

She ignored this and spoke to Leeman, who was standing up and looking sheepish. 'And you! What kind of a man are you? You let him hit Maria and did nothing but hit the floor when the gun went off. What a hero!'

He reddened angrily. 'Stow it, you bitch, or I'll do you.'

'Oh, fine. Bold as brass now, are we?'

He made a move towards her, but Diaz said sharply: 'Leave her. She is nothing. We have other business to attend to.' He looked at

Payne. 'I do not believe you have been telling the truth.'

'In what way?'

'I believe you do have the diamond with you. You are just pretending that you have not.'

'You can believe what you wish. But it happens to be the truth.'

'We will see about that. Raggler!'

'Yes, Mr Diaz?' Raggler said, looking at him nervously.

'Search him.'

Raggler hesitated, apparently uncertain whether or not to obey this order.

'Oh, come along,' Payne said. 'Get it over with. I won't break your arm this time.'

'Well, if you don't mind—'

'It makes no difference whether he minds or not,' Diaz snapped. 'Do it.'

Raggler, none too happily, made the search, Payne helping him and mocking him at the same time. He found no diamond.

Raggler spoke apologetically to Diaz. 'Sorry, Mr D. Nothing there. He's clean.'

Payne turned his mockery on Diaz. 'You see, Colonel? You shouldn't judge everybody by your own standards. Some of us tell the truth.'

Diaz sneered. 'Indeed! And now perhaps you will tell me some more of the truth. Where have you hidden it?'

'The Emperor Stone? Oh, in a very safe place.'

'Where is this safe place?'

'That is something I'm afraid you'll have to guess, because I don't intend to tell you.'

'Don't be stupid,' Diaz said. 'You see this pistol in my hand. I can make you tell me.' He pointed the weapon at Payne and his forefinger was curled about the trigger. 'Do you wish to be shot?'

'Mr Diaz!' Raggler begged. 'Mr Diaz, don't!'

'Don't let it bother you, Raggler,' Payne said. 'He won't shoot me. He's not going to kill the goose that he hopes will lay the golden egg. Are you, Colonel?'

Diaz gave his teeth-baring wolfish grin. 'No, I am not. But perhaps the girlfriend will tell me what I want to know.'

'No,' Payne said quickly. 'Joanna knows nothing. She can't tell you.'

'Never mind. It doesn't matter whether she knows or not. All that's needed is a lever, and she will serve the purpose. You take my meaning, Payne?'

Payne did. What Diaz was suggesting was that a bit of work on Joanna would persuade him to talk, because he would not be able to keep his secret and watch her being tortured.

Raggler was looking worried again. This sort of thing was outside his experience. Gathering evidence in divorce cases, looking for missing persons, sniffing out information on this and that, standing around in the rain, getting wet feet and colds in the head, yes. It was all in his usual day's work. But violence, firing guns, torturing people to make them talk; none of this was really his line of country. He had been drawn into this business by the promise of good money, but he had not realised where it might lead and he was not happy with the way matters were developing, not happy at all.

'Mr Diaz,' he said. 'Really, I don't think—'

Diaz ignored him and spoke to Leeman. 'Suppose you were to twist her arm—just for a start. Do you think you could do that?'

Leeman hesitated, looking at Joanna doubtfully and then back at Diaz. 'Well, I—'

'You want your money, don't you? Your share.'

So, Payne thought, Leeman was being bribed as well as threatened. Perhaps he had decided that half a loaf was better than no bread and that if Diaz was going to get the diamond anyway he might as well earn a bit by helping him.

'You bet I want it. I bin co-operating, ain't I?'

'Then continue to co-operate. Do as I tell you or you may not get anything. Except perhaps a bullet in the brain. If you aren't willing to help me you'll be better out of the way.'

It was the threat coming up again, and it settled the argument as far as Leeman was concerned. He said hurriedly: 'No need for that. I'll do it.'

He moved towards Joanna, but she was not waiting for him. He was between her and the door, preventing her from making an escape that way, but she dodged behind the sofa.

'Keep away from me, you bastard! Don't you dare lay your filthy hands on me!'

He took no notice of the protest. He chased her round the sofa and caught her very quickly, seizing her left arm. But she was more of a handful than he had expected; she hit him in the face with her clenched fist and kicked him on the shin. It served only to rouse his temper, and he was no longer half-hearted in his assault on her.

'All right, you bitch! You've asked for it and now you'll get it.'

She continued to struggle, but he was the stronger and he gave a savage twist to the arm which made her scream. It was obviously hurting her a lot and Maria put in a word of protest and pleading.

'Garry! Please! Don't do it, Garry!'

She might as well have saved her breath; he was not listening. He was ready enough now to do all that Diaz wanted him to do and maybe more. It was evident that there was a vicious streak in him, and it had been brought out by the girl's spirited resistance.

Raggler was looking on with increasing dismay, but he was not making any move to intervene. It was time, Payne decided, for him to take a hand. Diaz was still pointing the pistol at him, but he was confident that the man would not shoot because he needed him alive. So he made a dart at Leeman. Diaz tried to block his path but was brushed aside, and in another moment he had whipped an arm round Leeman's neck and was hauling him away from Joanna.

Leeman was making choking noises and trying to free himself from the arm that was pressing on his throat and stopping his breathing, but he was having no success.

'Cool it, Garry,' Payne said, speaking close to Leeman's ear, so that there was no possibility of his not hearing. 'Calm down or maybe I'll finish you. I could strangle you, you know. Easy.'

He was not kidding; it was the truth. He had a lock on Leeman and might even have broken his neck. It would not have grieved him greatly to have done either of these things, but in the event he did neither, because something hard struck him on the side of the head and everything for him was blacked out as though the darkness of the grave had suddenly come upon him.

CHAPTER THIRTEEN

RIDE

He came to with Leeman splashing cold water in his face from a polythene bowl.

'You can stop that,' he said. 'You're making my clothes sopping wet.'

Leeman stopped what he was doing and stepped back. 'You ought to be grateful. You damn near croaked me.'

'Pity I didn't finish the job.'

He guessed that he had not been out for long, but during that time the situation had changed somewhat, and not at all in his favour. He was now tied to an upright chair and his head was throbbing and he felt sick. Later he was to learn that Diaz had hit him with the pistol; that was why his head was so sore. But the blow had been a shrewd one, with just enough power in it to knock him out for a short while but to do no serious damage.

Diaz had known precisely what he was doing and had done it with considerable skill. He had had no wish to turn the victim into a hospital case, which was something that was always likely to happen when a person was rapped on the head with a hard object and some force. The ordinary man was not constructed like those cast-iron heroes of adventure films who could be struck in the upper storey with baseball bats or pickaxe handles and yet come up a couple of minutes later as right as rain and ready to dish out some of the same treatment to the opposition. Normal people got cracked skulls and concussion, and might be sent into a coma for months on end. Diaz wanted none of that, however bad-tempered he might be feeling. He needed Payne alive and well and fit enough to lead to where the diamond was stowed away. So he had moderated the blow accordingly.

Payne was alive and as well as could be expected, even if he was not feeling as chipper as he might have wished. He was still in the same room, and Diaz, Leeman, Raggler and Joanna were all there; the girl tied to another chair. Only Maria was missing. He noted this fact as soon as his head cleared a little. It was Diaz who provided the information to explain this absence.

'Miss Cardona is for the present under restraint.'

'Restraint?'

'She is locked in an upstairs room. It seemed advisable. She would not wish to be a witness to what is about to happen if you refuse to co-operate. It might distress her.'

Payne did not need to be told what was going to happen if he still declined to play things Diaz's way: it would be some more of the treatment he had temporarily put a stop to before being slugged.

He spoke to Joanna. 'Are you all right?'

'Does it look as if I am?' She sounded out of temper. Angry with him perhaps for getting her into this fix.

'The young lady has taken no harm—yet,' Diaz said. 'What the immediate future may hold is another matter. She could suffer a great deal of pain if we meet with further obstinacy on your part. So now I ask you again, are you ready to reveal where you have put the diamond?'

Payne said nothing.

'Very well. I can see that you are a very stubborn man. So be it.'

He made a sign to Leeman, who moved towards Joanna. Payne saw that he now had a small object in his right hand. It was a razor blade. He paused when he was close enough to the girl to be able to reach out and touch her. She was staring at the razor-blade in obvious terror.

'No, Garry! No, you wouldn't!'

Leeman glanced at Diaz, waiting for further orders.

Diaz spoke to Payne. 'You know what will happen. He will make incisions. She will bleed; but bleeding is nothing. It ends. What does not end is the after-effect, the hideous scarring. She will be disfigured for life. Her good looks will be ruined. Do you want that?'

Joanna looked at Payne. It was a mute

appeal to him not to let this happen to her.

Still he said nothing.

'I am surprised,' Diaz said. 'I expected more nobility from you, more humanity. You disappoint me, Payne.'

He gave another signal to Leeman. Joanna screamed, but the blade had not touched her.

Payne broke his silence. 'Stop!'

Leeman checked his hand an inch from the girl's face.

'I'll tell you what you want to know,' Payne said. 'The diamond is in my hotel room.'

'In your hotel room!' Diaz stared at him in disbelief. 'No; that is impossible. You would never have left it there. Why, anyone could have walked in and picked it up. It would have been a crazy thing to do. You are lying.'

'I am not lying. And no one will pick it up because it is too well hidden. I am not a fool.'

Diaz took a long hard look at Payne and said: 'Well, I suppose I shall have to take your word for that. Where is this hotel?'

Payne told him.

'We shall have to go there. And I hope for your sake and the young lady's that you are telling the truth. I shall not be at all happy if I am being misled.'

'I am not misleading you,' Payne assured him. 'Where would be the point? You would find out and we would be back to square one.'

'Yes, that is so; I will certainly find out. Because now that you have told us where the hotel is Mr Leeman will take me there in his car to get the diamond while Mr Raggler stays here to keep an eye on you.'

Payne shook his head. 'I don't think that would be at all a good plan.'

'Why not?'

'They wouldn't give you the key to my room for a start. Or if you did manage to persuade them to let you have it, you still wouldn't find the diamond. As I told you, it's well hidden.'

'But you will tell us where to look.'

'I could do that, but you might have a lot of difficulty just the same. Your best bet would be to take me with you. That would make everything much easier.'

Diaz regarded him with deep suspicion. 'You are not, I hope, planning to do something clever; which might be far from clever really. Because if we do take you along with us you have to remember that I shall have the gun, and I shall not hesitate to use it if you cause the slightest bit of trouble. You understand that, don't you?'

'I understand it perfectly. I know you're not the man to fool around with.'

'And you will remember also that the girls will still be here. Their safety depends on your good behaviour, and I am sure you would not wish to be the cause of anything unpleasant happening to them.'

'You don't need to spell it out. I know the score. Frankly, I won't really be sorry to be shot of the diamond. All it's given me so far is a load of trouble. Maybe after this you'll be the one who has the trouble.'

Diaz smiled faintly. 'That is a risk I am prepared to take.'

* * *

Leeman's car was a red Jaguar, which he drove with a kind of bravado, as if it were an extension of his own personality. He seemed to regard all other drivers as either nitwits or villains who ought never to have been allowed to occupy space on the roads, which in an ideal world would have been constructed for his exclusive use.

Payne and Diaz rode in the back, the latter with the pistol ready to hand in case his companion should have thoughts of making an attempt at escape. In fact he had no cause for concern on this point, for Payne had no intention of trying anything of the sort. He was perfectly relaxed on the journey, and if there was any worrying to be done he left that to Diaz, and perhaps Leeman as well.

He did, however, indulge in a little goading of Leeman. 'You know, Garry, that you're backing the wrong horse, don't you? I don't know how much Colonel Diaz has promised you as a reward for your help, but I can guarantee that once he's got his hands on the diamond he'll be away like a shot out of a gun and leave you to whistle for your money.'

'Shut your mouth,' Leeman answered in a surly tone. He seemed to be in a bad mood.

And Diaz said: 'You will accomplish nothing by trying to blacken me in Mr Leeman's eyes. He knows he will get more from me than he would from you.'

'Well, you would say that, wouldn't you? But can he be sure? That's the question. What does he know about you? A foreigner, a dago, and maybe a thief and a traitor.'

This seemed to touch Diaz on the raw, and he responded angrily: 'Hold your tongue. You are asking to be killed. I am a man of honour and I will not be insulted like this.'

Payne gave a derisive laugh but said nothing more.

* * *

They had left Joanna at the house, locked in the room where Maria had already been confined. They were both prisoners, with Raggler acting as warder. It was not a role for which he had any liking; Payne had the impression that he would have been glad to wash his hands of the whole business; but he had allowed himself to become involved and was too much under the thumb of Colonel Diaz to walk away now. And for him too there was no doubt the promise of more money to come.

Leeman knew the way; he had travelled it many times and was never at a loss. They passed through Leytonstone, and by then a light rain had set in, drifting on to the windscreen and making it necessary to start the wipers going. Hackney Marshes were left on the right and then Victoria Park on the left, and soon they were in the heart of London, contending with the evening traffic. Eventually Leeman brought the car on to the Bayswater Road and soon after that he was taking directions from Payne for the final part of the journey.

The hotel had an unimposing front entrance. Indeed, it looked what it was: one of the less fashionable of the capital's establishments of accommodation. But simple as it was, it satisfied Payne's demands; he was not seeking anything lavish, and besides, he was not planning to stay there for long.

He picked up his key from the desk in the lobby, and the receptionist seemed more interested in the paperback novel she was reading than in his two companions. She made no remark when he led them up the stairs, and in a moment they came to his room on the first floor. Here he unlocked the door, pushed it open and ushered Diaz and Leeman inside. He then closed and again locked the door.

'So that we are not disturbed.'

He noticed that Diaz was now holding the gun in his right hand. Entering the hotel he had kept it in his jacket pocket, but his hand had been in the pocket also and Payne had had no doubt that he was gripping the weapon even then.

The room was not large; with three men in it, it became a trifle crowded. It was simply furnished with a single bed, a wardrobe, a dressing-table and one chair. There was a wash-basin fixed to one wall, with hot and cold taps, both rather tarnished. Illumination was provided by an electric light in the middle of the ceiling, and there was another one on a cabinet by the bed.

Payne walked to the window and drew the curtains across, aware that Diaz was watching him closely.

'Well?' Diaz said. 'Where is it?' He sounded impatient. There was a hungry eagerness in him that he could hardly control.

Payne indicated the wash-basin with a pointing finger. 'It is behind that.'

'What do you mean, behind that? How can it be?'

'There is a cavity in the wall where some plaster has come out.'

'And you left it in there?'

'Why not? Who would look in such an unlikely place?'

'You are mad,' Diaz said. 'Anyone might. A maid cleaning the basin, a plumber, a thief.'

'Most unlikely. I am sure it's still there.'

'Then take it out, take it out. What are you

waiting for?'

Payne looked at him mockingly. 'My, what a state you're in! You can't wait to get your hands on it, can you? While I for my part am in no hurry at all.'

'Damn you!' Diaz was almost frothing at the mouth. 'Get it. Get it and give it to me.'

'Oh, very well, since you want it so badly,' Payne said. He moved to the wash-basin, bent down and probed under it with his hand. 'Yes, it is still there. I can feel it.'

'So bring it out.' Diaz could not keep still; he was shaking with excitement.

Leeman was eager too, though he was hanging back. He seemed to have caught some of Diaz's fever now that he was so close to setting eyes on this valuable gem of which he had so far only heard.

Payne withdrew his hand and straightened up. 'No. It's for you to take it out. I wouldn't want to rob you of the delight.'

'What nonsense is this?' Diaz stared at him, suspicion immediately aroused. 'You are up to some trick. I do not believe it is in there. You are trying to fool me.'

'Not at all. I touched it with my fingers. Try for yourself. It will give you a thrill. You've worked hard enough to get it.'

'Stand aside then.' Diaz was still suspicious, but eagerness to take the diamond in his hand was overwhelming.

Payne moved back from the wash-basin and

Diaz took his place, keeping the pistol in his right hand still pointing at Payne. He too had to stoop to get his left hand under the basin and grope about for the hole in the plaster which he had been assured was there.

'I can find nothing.'

'Reach higher,' Payne said. 'Your hand is too low. Between the wall and the basin. There is a gap. Can't you feel it?'

Almost imperceptibly as he was speaking he had moved closer to Diaz. The colonel, still groping, took his attention off Payne for a moment and was lost. Payne grabbed his right forearm and slammed his wrist against the edge of the wash-basin, while in the same instant he snatched the pistol from Diaz's loosening grip. Quickly he sprang back and covered Diaz with the gun, which was in fact a Beretta .32, a deadly weapon at close quarters.

'Don't try anything, Colonel.'

Diaz was standing up, cursing, holding his injured wrist. Leeman had not moved.

Diaz glared at Payne in fury. 'You lied. There is no diamond behind that basin.'

'No, of course there isn't. Would I really be stupid enough to leave it in such a place? As you yourself remarked, anyone could have found it.'

'So where is it? Where have you hidden it, damn you?'

'Now why would I tell you that?'

'You will pay for this deception.' Diaz was

still in a rage but was trying to be cool. 'You think you have been very clever, but it will not help you. I shall get the diamond in the end and you will wish you had never played games with me.'

'That remains to be seen. But now it's time we were on our way. There's no point in staying here any longer. You go first, Garry, and mind you behave yourself.'

'Where are we going?' Leeman asked. He appeared subdued and confused. Payne guessed that he was wondering which way to jump. Diaz no longer looked so good a bet.

'We'll go back to your place. Then we'll work something out.'

After they had left the room he locked the door, keeping Diaz covered with the pistol. He felt pretty certain Leeman would do as he was told, but the colonel needed watching. They went down the stairs with Leeman in the lead and Payne bringing up the rear. He had the gun in his pocket now, but his hand was on it. He handed in the key at the desk, and the receptionist looked faintly surprised to see him leaving again so soon with the other two men, but she said nothing.

The Jaguar was where they had left it, and Leeman unlocked the door and got into the driver's seat. Payne and Diaz got into the back, and it was as it had been on the way in, except that Payne was now the one with the gun and Diaz the prisoner. Diaz was saying nothing, but he was probably thinking a lot. Payne was thinking too, because he still had a problem and could not see quite how it was going to be worked out. He would just have to play it by ear and see how things went.

Diaz was silent all the way through the West End and the City, and Leeman was concentrating on his driving. Payne felt disinclined to start anything in the way of conversation, so the journey was a pretty quiet one. Until they reached Whitechapel. Here there was a brief hold-up in the traffic and Diaz decided to make a run for it.

He had the door open and was out of the car before Payne realised what he was doing, and then it was too late to take preventive action. He thought of giving chase and then thought better of it. The fact was that he was not really sorry to see the back of the colonel, who would have been something of a bother to him when they reached Leeman's place. The question would have been what to do with him, but his escape had given the answer to that particular problem.

Leeman had turned his head and was looking questioningly at Payne. 'You going after him?'

'No,' Payne said. 'Good riddance to the bastard.' He pulled the door shut. Diaz had taken the first side-turning he had come to and was already out of sight. 'Let's be on our way.'

The blockage had cleared and traffic was moving again. The Jaguar moved with it.

CHAPTER FOURTEEN

JOKERS

Raggler seemed uneasy when only the two of them walked in.

'Where's Mr Gonzalez? Mr Diaz, that is.'

'I think he suddenly remembered an urgent appointment,' Payne said. 'We were in Whitechapel and he opened the car door and beat it in a hurry without even saying goodbye.'

'Taking the diamond with him?'

'There wasn't no diamond,' Leeman said. 'Our friend here was just having us on, waiting for a chance to turn the tables. Which he did.'

Raggler looked puzzled. 'I don't get it.'

'What don't you get? It's plain bloody English, ain't it?' Leeman spoke sourly. He was probably wondering how it was all going to pan out for him, and maybe beginning to speculate whether he would get any profit from it or nothing but a dead loss. 'He took Diaz's gun off him, di'n't he?'

'But the diamond. What about the diamond?'

'There wasn't one. Don't you listen to anything I say? It was just a have, that about it being in the hotel room.' Leeman turned to Payne. 'You were planning to take him off guard, weren't you? You were planning it all along, right from the word go.'

'I did have something of the sort in mind,' Payne admitted.

'So what happens now?'

'Now we let the girls out. I suppose you have the key to their room, Mr Raggler?'

'Oh, yes.'

'And I hope that nothing unpleasant has happened to them while you've been their jailer. I shall hold you responsible if anything has.'

Raggler hastened to reassure him on this point. 'They're all right. I took them some refreshment and they're fine.'

'Go and fetch them then.'

'Yes, Mr Payne; anything you say.' Raggler seemed only too eager to please now that Payne had taken the upper hand. The knowledge that he had Diaz's pistol might have helped to persuade the private eye that he had better not make any trouble.

After a minute or two he came back, accompanied by the hostages. They too appeared surprised not to see Diaz. Payne explained the situation briefly.

'So you don't know where Diaz is now?' Joanna said.

'No idea. The last I saw of him he was making a fast getaway.'

'And empty-handed?'

'Yes, empty-handed and in a filthy temper.'

'What do you think he'll do now?'

'There's not much he can do.'

'He won't give up,' Maria said. 'He's not that sort of man.'

'Well, we shall see.'

Leeman was hanging around, looking uncomfortable and watching Joanna uneasily. She seemed to notice him suddenly, and she walked up to him and gave him a stinging slap on the cheek.

'Pig!'

'Here!' he said. 'What was that for?'

'You know damn well what for. You were going to slash my face with a razor blade. Remember?'

'Aw, that was just fooling. I never would've done it.'

'Like hell, you wouldn't! You scum! You would have done anything Diaz told you to do.'

'No. It ain't true. I knew Alan would cave in before I could touch you.'

'And suppose he hadn't. What then?'

'Then I'd have told Mr Diaz it was no go.'

'You're a liar, Garry. You're a liar and a crook and a damned coward into the bargain.'

He seemed about to deny the charges, but then appeared to realise it would be a waste of breath. He turned away from her and slumped down in one of the armchairs.

Maria spoke to Payne. 'What will you do with the diamond now?'

'You still won't take it?'

'No.'

'Then I shall have to give some more thought to the problem. What about you? Do you intend staying here?'

'Oh, no. I couldn't now. Not after what has happened. Joanna and I have talked things over and I'm going back with her. For the present at least.'

Leeman pricked up his ears at this. 'So you're leaving?'

'Yes.'

'Well, that's nice, that is. Don't I get any say in the matter? You live off me as long as it suits you, and then as soon as you feel like it you walk out. No explanation, nothing. That really is nice.'

She looked at him with contempt. 'Do you need an explanation? Do I have to tell you that I can see now how stupid I was to be dazzled by your charm in the first place? Joanna warned me, but I wouldn't listen. I didn't want to hear the truth about you. But I'm not blind any more; I can see for myself what you are.'

'Oh, really?' Leeman was sneering. 'And what am I, may I ask?'

'Everything Joanna said you were, and more. This last business capped the lot. After the way you've acted do you imagine I could ever live with you again?'

'Okay,' he said, flaring up. 'Go. Get to hell out of here, you stupid bitch. Don't imagine I'll shed any tears. I'll be well shot of you. I managed all right before you came along and I'll manage when you're gone.'

'Even without the diamond?' Payne asked.

Leeman scowled at him. 'I reckon you'll hang on to it now. Like you meant to all along. You don't fool me. This has worked out just the way you wanted, ain't it?'

'If you want to think that, you're welcome.' Payne turned to Maria. 'How long will it take you to pack your things?'

'They are already packed,' she said. 'Everything was in the room where we were locked in, and Joanna helped me.'

'Then I think we'll be on our way. Mr Raggler, you've got a car here. Would you mind giving us a lift?'

Raggler made no objection. He had obviously decided that it was in his best interests to keep on the right side of Payne. He had given his assistance in some very shady business and he might have been apprehensive of coming up against the forces of the law if he did not take care.

'Not at all, Mr Payne. Be glad to oblige. Just tell me where you want to go and I'm your man.'

*   *   *

Travelling in Raggler's ageing Fiat was rather different from doing the same journey in Leeman's Jaguar. Raggler was a cautious driver and was not likely to be pulled up for speeding. They went first to the maisonette in Fulham, where Payne helped to carry Maria's luggage inside, having told the private eye to wait for him.

He did not stay long. Now that Maria was back in residence he felt a trifle superfluous, and he also had a feeling that there would be no more sightseeing with Miss Parrish for him. His regrets were minimal; Joanna had been a pleasant companion, but nothing more. He had never contemplated falling in love with her and he doubted whether she had had any ideas of that sort either.

'I'll call round in the morning,' he said. 'For a talk.' There was still the question of what to do with the diamond. He wished Maria would take it; she was really making things difficult for him. But perhaps they would be able to work something out.

'Thank you for all you've done,' she said. 'I've been a terrible nuisance to you, haven't I?'

So she realised that. Well, it was something.

'Don't give it a thought,' he said.

Raggler was waiting for him in the Fiat.

'It's odd the way things turn out, isn't it, Mr Payne? There was me, hanging around trying to find out where you were staying, and now I know and it's not worth a bean to me.'

'That's how it goes. You win some and you lose some.'

'Fact is, I never did go a lot on that there Diaz. Calling hisself Gonzalez and all.'

'Let it be a lesson to you. And if he comes round asking you to help him again, show him the door.'

'I will. You can rely on me for that.'

Payne doubted whether he could rely on Raggler for anything, but he did not say so. What he did say was:

'I hope he paid you something for your trouble.'

'Well, there was a retainer. But I was supposed to get a lot more if things turned out right. I can say goodbye to that now, I reckon.'

'I reckon you can.'

*   *   *

He called at the maisonette in Fulham at about eleven o'clock the next morning, figuring that the girls might not be up early after the events of the previous day. But he did not get round to pressing the bell-push because his attention was caught by a note attached to the front door by four drawing-pins.

It was a brief note written in block capitals, and it was an order really, telling him to call the telephone number which followed. It was signed: Joanna.

He did not like it. From the wording it was

obvious that the girls were not in the house. Nevertheless, he tried the door and found it was locked. Then he did ring the bell, but there was no response, and that was that. They were just not there.

There was no sense to it. What had made them decide to go out so early in the day? After all, they knew he was coming to see them. What urgent business could have cropped up that had to be attended to at such short notice? And why the telephone number to ring? He glanced at it again, and he liked it none the better this second time. It seemed to mock him, and he had a feeling that when he rang the number he would hear a familiar voice coming down the line and pouring into his ear; a voice he did not at all wish to hear.

But he had to make the call; he could not simply walk away and leave it. So he tore the note from the door, stuffed it into his pocket and went to find a telephone-box.

There was no delay in getting a reply when he dialled the number, they had evidently been waiting for his call. And it was the voice he had expected.

'That you, Alan?' Leeman said.

'It's me. What lark are you up to now?'

'Not one you're going to like very much.' Even over the telephone the gloating note was evident in Leeman's voice. 'We got the girls, and now we got you on the hook.'

'So Diaz is with you?'

'Sure he is.'

It was what might have been expected. He should have known Diaz would not give up; Maria had told him so and she had been right. He must have made his way back to Leeman's place at some time after the rest of them had left in Raggler's car; and the two of them had put their heads together and come up with a new plan. Then they must have driven to Fulham in the Jaguar and kidnapped the girls. It had probably not been too difficult, especially if Diaz had got himself another gun; and maybe Leeman had been able to supply that.

Payne felt angry with himself for not foreseeing that something of this kind might happen. He should have warned the girls; warned them not to open the door to anyone. But he had not thought of it, and now Diaz had seized the advantage again.

'Do you want to speak to him?' Leeman asked.

'Not especially.'

'Well, he wants to speak to you. Hang on.'

Payne hung on, and a moment later Diaz's harsh voice was assailing his ear.

'Now listen, Payne. We have Miss Cardona and Miss Parrish, and no harm will come to them if you do exactly as I tell you.'

'You've got them with you there?'

'No, not here. So don't have any bright ideas of rescuing them. They are in a safe place where you will not find them. And do not bring in the police, because that could be fatal—and I mean fatal. You understand?'

'I understand.'

It was a threat to kill the hostages, and coming from a man like Diaz it had to be taken seriously.

'But do not worry. They will be perfectly well if you follow my instructions. Tonight you will bring the diamond to the Hungerford Bridge walkway. Midnight—no make it one o'clock—halfway across. I will meet you there and you will give me the diamond. I will then telephone Leeman and instruct him to release the women and take them back to their house. Right?'

'How do I know you'll keep your side of the bargain?'

'You may accompany me when I make the call. Besides, what would I stand to gain by not setting them free once I have what I want?'

Payne could see the logic of that. And for his own part he would not be altogether sorry to conclude the whole wretched business in this way. He had no wish to let Diaz come out a winner; it galled him; but there seemed to be little alternative. With the girls stowed away in some secret place, which Leeman had no doubt provided, he had to act according to Diaz's instructions; it would be folly to put their lives at risk for the sake of one damned diamond, however valuable.

'Do you agree?' Diaz asked.
'Yes, I agree.'
'And no tricks this time?'
'No tricks.'
'Good.'
He heard the click as Diaz put the telephone down. It seemed to him to be an oddly triumphant sound. Diaz had won.

*   *   *

He went back to his quarters and asked for the parcel he had deposited in the hotel safe. It was a small cardboard box wrapped in brown paper and sealed with sticky tape. He took it to his room and cut it open and removed the diamond. Again he was struck by the beauty of the stone as it lay in the palm of his hand, sparkling with a kind of inner fire.

For a moment he had an almost irresistible desire to hang on to it, not to sell but to keep for the sheer delight of owning such an object; to be able to handle it, to look at it, to luxuriate in its glittering opulence. But the moment passed and he dropped the jewel into his pocket.

There were several hours to be got through before the time of his rendezvous with Diaz and he had no wish to hang around in the uninspiring hotel room, so he went out again. He spent some time strolling aimlessly in Hyde Park and Kensington Gardens. It was a cool day, overcast but dry. A few leaves were already dropping from the trees and soon the flower-beds might be ravaged by frost. Maybe there would be snow before Christmas. He had not seen any snow for years and he remembered how he had delighted in it as a boy, tobogganing and making snowmen which melted into shapeless heaps of slush when the thaw came. So long ago.

Evening found him in the West End, still killing time, a fortune in his pocket. Suppose he were to be mugged now and the diamond taken from him! Would Diaz believe such a story? It was doubtful. But he was not really afraid of mugging. For one thing he had the pistol which he had lifted from the man, and he knew how to take care of himself. He had certainly had enough experience.

He had a meal in Soho and went to a cinema. At a quarter to one he was on the Victoria Embankment and approaching Hungerford Bridge. He had read somewhere that the original Hungerford Suspension Bridge had been taken down in Victorian times and parts of it had been used in the construction of the Clifton Suspension Bridge over the River Avon. It had been replaced by the Charing Cross Railway Bridge, and the walkway had been erected alongside it for the use of pedestrians. It seemed an odd place for Diaz to choose for their meeting, but perhaps Leeman had suggested it for some reason. On the other hand Diaz might have known about it anyway;

Payne remembered hearing that in his younger days he had spent some years in London as a student, and no doubt he had come to know the Metropolis pretty well. He might even have visited the Festival Hall on occasion, crossing over from Charing Cross Station.

At five to one Payne was at what he judged to be the approximate midway point of the bridge, hedged in on each side by the tall fencing which would have made it difficult for a prospective suicide to throw himself into the water flowing below. A train rattled by on the railway bridge, lights showing, but few people seemed to be using the footbridge at that time of night. He came to a halt and waited.

Diaz arrived almost on the stroke of one o'clock, walking briskly but making scarcely any sound.

'So,' he said, 'you are here.'

'Did you think I wouldn't be?'

'It would have been foolish of you if you had not been. I assume you have the diamond?'

'Yes.'

'Give it me then and let us have done with this business.'

It was apparent that he was suppressing his eagerness with extreme difficulty. Payne felt inclined to play with him for a while longer, but there would have been no point in it. He dipped a hand into his pocket and brought out the stone.

Diaz gave a kind of sigh as he saw it. 'Ah!' He

stretched out his left hand, palm uppermost. Payne laid the diamond on the waiting palm and Diaz closed his hand on it, grasping the prize at last.

'And now,' he said, 'there is just one further piece of business to be attended to.'

Payne imagined he was referring to the telephone call, but it was not that. Diaz's right hand had been in his jacket pocket, but now he drew it out and there was a small pistol in it. Payne was not surprised that he should be armed, even though he had lost the Beretta; what did surprise him was that he should have brought the weapon out now. It was Diaz himself who supplied the reason.

'I warned you,' he said. 'I told you you would pay for your trickery and your insults. I am not a man to forgive an injury or hand out idle threats. I am going to kill you.'

'That would be a damned crazy thing to do. What would you gain by it?'

'Satisfaction.' There was venom in Diaz's voice, and gloating. He knew he had won and he was enjoying his triumph.

Another man might have been content with that; might have been happy to take his winnings and go. But Payne knew that Diaz would not do this; it was the plain truth he had spoken when he had said that he never forgave an injury. Payne was again angered with himself for a lack of foresight; he had the Beretta in his pocket and he should have had it out, ready for any treacherous move by the other man. But he had not; he had allowed a feeling of security to betray him; and now it seemed that he was about to pay for this carelessness with his life.

The thing was to keep Diaz talking; maybe then he could slide his hand unobtrusively into his pocket and haul out the Beretta before the colonel could shoot him. Or maybe he could shoot from the pocket. Maybe. It was all very much maybe.

'But surely,' he said, 'a man like you, a man of superior intelligence, would not put himself in danger for the sake of a momentary satisfaction.' He was moving his right hand now, almost imperceptibly, towards the pocket where the gun was waiting. 'It would be utter stupidity, a messy business, and you might be caught and arrested.'

'No chance of that,' Diaz said. 'There is no one near to witness the shooting. Few people use this bridge at this hour.'

That was true. It was no doubt the reason why it had been chosen. He could appreciate now the shrewdness of that choice. Here one might call in vain for help. And if anyone did come along the bridge it was pretty certain whoever it was would not interfere; people tended to steer clear of trouble if they could.

'So you thought of that. It was why you chose this place for a late night rendezvous, wasn't it? Clever of you, Colonel.'

He was moving his hand closer to the pocket; it was almost there; another inch or two—

Diaz spoke sharply. 'Stop! Don't make another move!'

Payne arrested the movement of his hand and froze.

Diaz said sneeringly: 'Do you imagine I don't know what you are trying to do? You have my pistol in your pocket and you are hoping to get it out before I shoot you. But it will not work. And now I think the time has come. *Adios*, mercenary!'

Payne thought of throwing himself out of the line of fire; he thought of making a dive at Diaz, of knocking the pistol aside before the man could fire it; he thought of turning and running away. He made none of these moves; none of them would have been of any use; the bullet would have come too quickly, boring into his flesh.

But the bullet did not come. Instead, two jokers turned up from the pack and changed the entire aspect of the game. They came running up from behind Diaz; young men, a black and a white; running fast with a kind of skipping, dancing motion. Diaz heard them and turned, but not soon enough to save himself. The white one was in the lead and he had a knife in his hand. The knife went into Diaz and his left arm gave a spasmodic jerk, a sort of reflex movement like someone throwing a ball. But it was not a ball that was thrown; it was the diamond, the Emperor Stone.

It went in an arc and passed through one of the interstices of the fencing on the side opposite the railway bridge. Payne did not hear it hit the water; it must have made a very small sound; but he saw it go and knew that it was really lost now. It would sink into the Thames mud, and if it were ever dredged up no one would know; for who ever looked for diamonds in the scourings of that ancient river?

Diaz fell, and the man who had stabbed him wrenched the knife out and thrust it in again. He was laughing. The light was poor, but Payne saw that he had cropped hair and brass earrings, stone-washed jeans and trainers. The black had dreadlocks and the same kind of gear; and he was laughing too, a fluting giggling laugh. Payne guessed they were high on drugs—grass or coke or maybe heroin; it mattered not which; hyped-up muggers; nice people to meet on a lonely bridge in the middle of the Thames and the night. But they had saved his life.

Yet maybe not for long. The black also had a knife and he was coming at him now. He hauled out the Beretta and let the man see it.

'Hold it right there!'

The black stopped. He was not too stoned to know what a gun looked like, and it made him pause, even maybe think. The white had finished with Diaz, who was no longer moving. He was holding the knife in his hand, blood dripping from the blade. He had not picked up Diaz's pistol, though it was lying beside the body; maybe he despised guns.

The two of them stood there, looking at Payne, shifting their feet, their shoulders, their arms, their heads; not keeping still for a moment, but coming no nearer.

'You think we 'fraid that li'l peashooter?' the black said.

'You should be,' Payne said. 'It could kill you.'

'You jus' kiddin', man. Mebbe we do to you what we done to him.' He pointed at Diaz, lying in his own blood, horribly still.

'Try it.'

The black accepted the invitation and took half a step towards him. Payne shot him in the arm, and he let out a howl and dropped the knife.

In a way it had been an accident. Payne had been intending to scare him by sending a bullet past him but close enough to let him know he meant business. But his aim had not been quite accurate enough for that, and the bullet had in fact gone into the arm. It might have been no more than a graze or it might have been a bone-breaker; either way it had an instant effect on the two men; they turned and ran, leaving both the knives behind.

He was now left with Diaz; there was no one

else in sight on the bridge. He stooped and put a finger on Diaz's neck. There was no trace of a pulse and there was no sound of any breathing. There was a lot of blood and it was evident that Diaz was as dead as a joint of beef on a butcher's slab.

There was no point in hanging around any longer and there was every reason to get away from there fast.

Payne did just that.

CHAPTER FIFTEEN

ALWAYS

He found a telephone-box and rang up a minicab firm and ordered a car to pick him up. He told the driver to take him out to Leeman's place.

'That's a long way,' the driver said. 'It'll cost you.'

'I don't give a damn what it costs. Just get me there.'

The driver took a good look at him and decided he was trustworthy. 'Okay, guv. Hop in.'

He paid off the cab-driver when they arrived at Leeman's. It was now getting on for three o'clock in the morning and chilly. He walked up the weedy drive and hammered on the front door with the iron knocker.

It was Leeman himself who opened the door. He was fully dressed and had probably been waiting up for a telephone call from Diaz. He looked scared when he saw who it was on the doorstep. It could have been the gun in Payne's hand that really frightened him.

'You!'

'Yes, me. Surprised?'

Leeman seemed to be struck dumb. He could only stare at Payne in disbelief. Perhaps he had known that Diaz intended killing this man now confronting him and very much alive. Or maybe he had guessed as much without being told.

'We'd better go inside,' Payne said. 'No sense in hanging around out here. It's too bloody cold.'

He pushed past Leeman and went straight to the sitting-room where the lights were on. Leeman closed the front door and followed him.

'Where are they, Garry?'

'Where are who?' Leeman asked.

'The girls, of course. Joanna and Maria.'

'How would I know?'

'Now don't fool around, Garry, you stupid bastard. Of course you know. You told me over the phone you'd got them. Remember?'

'Oh, did I? Well, I was just kidding.'

'And you're still kidding. Do you want me to shoot you in the leg just to jog your memory?

Diaz was supposed to ring you up as soon as he got the diamond to tell you to let them go. But he won't be ringing anybody, I can assure you of that. You can wait till Domesday and you'll never get a call from him, unless it's on the hot line from hell.'

Leeman's jaw dropped. 'You killed him?'

'No, I didn't kill him.'

'Then why—'

'He won't call because he can't call. And he won't be coming to see you again. So you can whistle for any money you were expecting from him. Now are you going to tell me where you've got the girls hidden away or do I have to start maiming you?'

He pointed the Beretta at Leeman's right knee, and his finger was on the trigger. But as he had expected there was no need to fire the pistol because Leeman decided there was no sense in holding out any longer.

'All right, all right. They're here.'

'In this house?'

'Yes.'

'But Diaz said they were somewhere else. A secret place.'

'Of course he did. But that was just to put you off coming here and trying to rescue them. It was a lie and you fell for it.'

Payne nodded. He might have guessed as much, but it had not even occurred to him. And even if it had he could not have been sure; he would have been obliged to go along with

Diaz's instructions anyway.

'All right then, you bastard. Go and get them.'

* * *

Leeman drove them back to the Fulham maisonette in the red Jaguar. He was very subdued and was maybe reflecting how things had all turned out to his disadvantage. Payne rode beside him and the girls were in the back. Nobody said much on the journey.

When they reached the end of the line Payne told Leeman to make himself scarce. 'I could have the police on to you if I felt like it, and then you'd be in dead trouble. Whether the girls will want to press charges, I can't say. Kidnapping is a serious crime, you know. But I don't think rubbish like you is worth bothering about. My advice, for what it's worth, is to keep your head down and your nose clean. On your way.'

He watched the Jaguar move away and he hoped it was the last he would ever see of Garry Leeman. Diaz's body would be found, of course, and there would be a murder investigation, but he felt quite sure Leeman would not step forward to offer information. He doubted whether Raggler would either. The private eye had had nothing to do with the kidnapping, but he had been involved in some dubious activities earlier and would have no desire to be interrogated by the police.

The two young muggers might be traced by fingerprints on the abandoned knives, but they would not be able to tell anything about Diaz or the diamond because they knew nothing.

That left only Joanna and Maria and himself. He followed them into the house for a heart-to-heart talk.

'You'll be wanting to know about Diaz and the Emperor Stone,' he said. 'I'd better tell you the whole story now. It won't take long, and then it won't come as such a shock when you read the papers or hear the news on radio or TV.'

They heard him out in silence. Then Maria said: 'So Diaz is dead and the diamond is gone.'

'Yes.'

'I am glad it is lost. It was an evil stone.'

'No,' Payne said. 'The evil was in those who possessed it or hoped to possess it. The stone itself was blameless; nothing but a lump of hardened carbon.'

He wondered what they would do now. Neither of them had a job and they had rent to pay and all the other expenses of living. But he supposed they would manage somehow, and it was not his responsibility.

They both kissed him when he said goodbye to them. They seemed to be grateful to him, though he could see no reason why Joanna should be, since he had only dragged her into a lot of trouble. But maybe it was because in a way he had rescued Maria from an unfortunate liaison and brought her back as a companion. It was not quite what he had set out to do, but in the end it was what he had done.

* * *

He met her at the airport and he was glad to see her, really glad. Relieved too, because even up to the last he had feared there might be some hitch that would prevent her coming.

He had written to her. In the letter he had told her that he loved her and wanted her to come to England and marry him. And it was not such a crazy idea at that, because although he had no job at present, he had some money. The greater part of the forty thousand dollars that Cardona had given him still remained, and over the years he had stowed away quite a useful amount from his earnings in solid investments. With this capital he would maybe set up in business on his own account. He had not yet decided what kind of business, but he would think of something. And possibly he could get a government grant. The future looked good.

Immediately he saw her his heart gave a leap and he knew that he had done the right thing. She was as lovely as he remembered her, or even more so; the one woman he really wanted.

'Welcome to England,' he said, and embraced her.

Outside it was a typical November day: overcast, shreds of fog hanging around, the kind of damp cold that penetrated to the bone.

'What charming weather!' she said. 'Is it always like this?'

'Always.'

'I'm going to love it,' she said. 'I just know I am. With you.'

We hope you have enjoyed this Large Print book. Other Chivers Press or G. K. Hall Large Print books are available at your library or directly from the publishers. For more information about current and forthcoming titles, please call or write, without obligation, to:

Chivers Press Limited
Windsor Bridge Road
Bath BA2 3AX
England
Tel. (01225) 335336

OR

G. K. Hall
P.O. Box 159
Thorndike, Maine 04986
USA
Tel. (800) 223–6121 (U.S. & Canada)
In Maine call collect: (207) 948–2962

All our Large Print titles are designed for easy reading, and all our books are made to last.